Tom Clancy's
Net Force Explorers:
Virtual Vandals

Created by Tom Clancy and Steve Pieczenik

First published in Great Britain in 1998
by HEADLINE BOOK PUBLISHING

A HEADLINE FEATURE paperback

10 9 8 7 6 5 4 3 2 1

ISBN 0 7472 6071 0

Typeset by
Letterpart Limited, Reigate, Surrey

Printed and bound in Great Britain by
Caledonian International Book Manufacturing Ltd, Glasgow

HEADLINE BOOK PUBLISHING
A division of Hodder Headline PLC
338 Euston Road
London NW1 3BH

Acknowledgments

We'd like to thank the following people, without whom this book would not have been possible: Bill McCay, for help in rounding out the manuscript; Martin H. Greenberg, Larry Segriff, Denise Little, and John Helfers at Tekno Books; Mitchell Rubenstein and Laurie Silvers at BIG Entertainment; Tom Colgan, of Putnam Books; Robert Youdelman, Esquire, and Tom Mallon, Esquire; and Robert Gottlieb of the William Morris Agency, agent and friend. We much appreciated the help.

Chapter 1

The April sky was a bright, cloudless blue, marked only by the thin white contrails of an aerospace plane's jet engines passing high above. Matt Hunter squinted his brown eyes, staring up from his seat in the Camden Yards stadium. *Must be just about ready to switch over to the rocket engines*, he figured.

An elbow in his right ribs brought his thoughts back to earth. 'Nice job on these seats, genius,' Andy Moore complained. 'We're going to broil out here in the sun today.' The blond boy ran a hand over the fair skin of his forehead. 'Anybody bring the sunblock?'

'Out of luck from this end, junior.' David Gray rolled back his shirtsleeves, exposing muscular brown arms. 'My sunblock comes courtesy of my African ancestors.' He shifted on his seat, however. 'You'd think that after renovating this place, they'd put some comfortable padding out here.'

Leif Anderson stretched back in his seat. 'It's comfortable enough from where I'm sitting.'

Matt gave his friend a look. The seat which Leif seemed to occupy was actually empty, the space filled with a

1

hologram. Leif was actually sitting in his parents' apartment in New York City, no doubt sprawled in a very expensive – and comfortable – computer-link chair. Implants beneath his skin connected him to the world Net, allowing his image to be seen here in Baltimore, while he experienced everything that was happening in the stadium nearly 200 miles away.

'You'd better tune up your sim a little, Anderson,' Matt joked. 'Otherwise, you won't be catching any hologram home runs.' To his other friends, both real and holo, he offered an embarrassed shrug. 'Hey, it's the first home game of the season for the Orioles. These were the best seats I could get.'

He shifted uncomfortably on the thinly padded bleacher seat. Any seat was worth the show they were about to see – and he didn't mean the baseball game. Matt and all his friends had an interest in anything to do with computers. They were fascinated with the global computer Net that ran so much of the world, and with Net Force, the organization which policed that computer webwork. That was why Matt, Leif, Andy, David and the others had joined the young people's auxiliary, the Net Force Explorers.

Getting in had not been easy – they'd had to survive a training course as tough as that faced by Marine recruits. (Not surprising, Matt thought. Net Force itself shared its roots with the Marines.) But they'd learned a lot more about computers than they could have hoped to find out anywhere else. In a world where operating a computer was more like flipping a light switch, Matt and his friends knew how the magic boxes *worked*.

The thing that had brought them to this game wasn't the

seats or the teams, but the stadium itself. Camden Yards had undergone a complete renovation, wiring in a huge computer system to operate a virtual reality – veeyar – simulator. Lots of sports arenas featured holographic projectors in the seats. But here, the whole field was set up for a huge-scale display.

Leif sat up a bit taller in his seat as the opposing teams finished their warm-ups. 'Here it comes,' he said.

An announcer's voice rumbled through the stadium. 'Welcome to the first home game of the Orioles' 2025 season. But we have *more* than just a great game waiting for you. No, you'll spend an inning in Baseball Heaven, thanks to our new veeyar system. Some of the all-time All-Stars of the game, the greatest sluggers in baseball history, will step into the batter's box against an ace pitcher and a dream defensive team. Can heavy hitting defeat great pitching and fielding? Let's find out!'

For a moment, a shadow seemed to fall across the field as the last of the live players trotted off. Then, eighteen ghostly figures swam into existence in front of the opposing dugouts. They wore a variety of uniforms, all of them old-fashioned to Matt's eyes, some of them belonging to teams that didn't exist anymore.

Some of the virtual players waved or tipped their caps to the crowd. Leif Anderson whistled and clapped. 'None of this is scripted,' he said. 'It's all being randomly generated by the system's computers, based on the players' records, the chances they took swinging and fielding, even the way they reacted to the fans.'

'Who's the fat guy on the Sluggers team?' Andy Moore asked.

Leif stared at Andy as if he'd burped out loud in church. 'That's Babe Ruth. The 1927 Babe Ruth – he hit sixty home runs that season. And a little farther down the line is Ty Cobb. He got on base more than 4,000 times in his career – and got into more fights with the fans than anyone else I ever heard of.'

'I hope you've got an info-dump whispering all this stuff in your ear,' Matt said. 'Because if you're blowing brain cells on hundred-year-old sports statistics . . .'

Leif just grinned. 'If you take a close look at those All-Stars out there, you'll notice that at least half of them are wearing the uniforms of New York teams – the Sluggers have Ruth and Lou Gehrig from the Yankees, Frankie Frisch from the old New York Giants, and Don Drysdale was with the Brooklyn Dodgers. The fielders have Joe DiMaggio and Bill Dickey from the Yankees, Keith Hernandez from the Mets, and Willie Mays and Christy Mathewson from the Giants. They all played for my hometown!'

'Big yawn,' Matt said just to annoy his friend. 'Why have they got all these ancient guys?'

'There was a cutoff – nobody who played in this century,' Leif replied. 'Some of these guys played into the 1980s, like Ozzie Smith, Mike Schmidt, and Johnnie Bench. Keith Hernandez played into the nineties.'

Matt laughed. 'What I want to see is how they play *now*.'

The All-Star defensive team took the field as one of the sluggers, a guy in a Philadelphia uniform, stepped up to the plate.

'One thing computer players don't need,' David Gray joked. 'Warm-up practice.'

'You got it,' Leif chuckled. 'Every pitch, every swing – strikeout or error, we'll see it because that player's number came up on the computers.' He leaned forward eagerly in his seat, yelling, 'Go, Mike!'

Glancing over at Matt, he said, 'Mike Schmidt. Serious slugger.'

Christy Mathewson mowed him down with three strikes. Next up was Ty Cobb, who managed to get a single. Lou Gehrig followed with a screaming line drive, captured by Roberto Clemente in a diving catch.

Babe Ruth was the clean-up batter on the Sluggers. He had an odd batting stance, his bat seeming to rest on his shoulder. That was how he stood while the great Mathewson whiffed two strikes right past him.

'Is this the Babe or the Blob?' Matt asked.

'Let's just see what the Bambino does,' Leif replied.

The virtual Babe Ruth stepped out of the batter's box, taking the bat off his shoulder. Then he simply pointed off into the bleachers, beyond the outfield.

Leif laughed out loud. 'That's a famous gesture. The Babe is showing where he intends to send the next pitch.'

At that moment, though, four figures rose from their seats in the top row of the center-field bleachers. It was as if they'd been waiting for Ruth's signal.

Matt wondered how he hadn't noticed them before. The quartet was dressed in costumes at least as old-fashioned as the uniforms on the holographic players. In fact, they looked like characters out of an ancient, black-and-white gangster flat-film, the sort of thing that had preceded entertainment holos.

Three of the weirdos were male figures, dressed in

pin-striped suits with broad-brimmed hats. The fourth was a striking-looking blond woman in a long skirt and an old-fashioned sweater, with a little hat perched on her head.

The tallest man in the little group pointed back at Babe Ruth. 'Ah, pipe down, ya big, fat slob!'

Matt frowned as Leif stood up, trying to get a better look at the hecklers. Ty Cobb went racing into the outfield, screaming insults back at the hecklers. Yet his voice was almost inaudible.

'Something is wrong here,' Matt said. 'We shouldn't have been able to hear that guy.'

Yet the taunting voice was still echoing throughout the stadium – as if the tall figure in the outfield had somehow taken over the public-address system. But that was impossible – wasn't it?

Matt was in for a worse surprise. What the foursome in the bleachers did next was *completely* impossible. They reached under their seats and pulled out guns – big guns, heavy guns . . . and, weirdly enough, guns as antique as the costumes the quartet was wearing.

Matt had only seen Thompson submachine guns in holos. They were big, heavy, clumsy things. But the four in the stands handled them as if they were light as feathers. The weapons thundered out as the intruders sprayed the field, cutting down the holographic ballplayers.

Joe DiMaggio couldn't outrun a machine-gun bullet. Nor could Willie Mays or Roberto Clemente. Ty Cobb was also cut down. The tallest of the gunners ignored the nearby, easy targets. He set his sights on Babe Ruth himself, sending the Yankee slugger flying back in an ungraceful dance of death.

Harsh laughter echoed across the field. 'Too easy!' the tall gunman hooted. 'The target was so big!'

They've got to be holo characters, Matt told himself. The drums on those machine guns can't hold more than a hundred rounds. And they *must* have fired at least twice that.

Holos or not, the quartet of thugs was emptying the stands. A huge V-shape in the bleachers had cleared as real and virtual spectators bolted from their seats to get out of the line of fire. Frightened people clogged the stairs and walkways, clawing at one another as they tried to flee.

Matt's lips twisted in a scornful smile as he watched the stampeding crowd. 'Some idiot is going to get his or her neck broken, running away from that little laser-show,' he began.

Then Matt noticed the still forms slumped in their seats all through the triangle of death.

He turned in sudden concern. 'Leif—' he began.

His friend had actually climbed up on his seat to get a better view of the chaos in the stands. He was still up there, a perfect target, as a hologram bullet passed through his chest.

Leif tumbled off the bleacher seat, his eyes wide, his mouth distorted in a silent scream. He landed soundlessly on the floor – not very realistic, Matt found himself thinking. But with all the mayhem going on, the stadium's veeyar simulation system was probably getting overloaded.

Matt pushed those thoughts away as he dropped to one knee, yelling, 'Anybody here in virtual, pull the plug! Get out of here!'

The holographic images of several of his friends, and

many of the strangers within earshot, quickly winked out. Matt barely noticed. All his attention was on his downed friend Leif. There was no sign of a bullet wound, Matt noted with a sigh of relief. But Leif definitely wasn't in very good shape.

His face seemed waxy, white as chalk. Leif's eyes were wide and staring, but they didn't show any signs of consciousness. The pupils had shrunk to pinpoint size.

Matt recognized the symptoms. Shock. It was a common response to physical or mental trauma. It was also a nerve problem when something went wrong with computer implants.

Basic training in the Net Force Explorers meant a full course in first aid. But there was nothing Matt could do to help his friend. Leif wasn't here, he was 200 miles away. Matt couldn't even get a pulse through the failing veeyar link.

He dug into his back pocket, hauling out his wallet. Flipping aside his IDs and Universal Credit Card, he came to the foilpack keypad that came with every wallet. Matt activated the power and hit the 'phone' option. The flexible circuitry inside the tough polymer material switched to the pre-coded cellular phone format.

Matt muttered a brief prayer as he held the wallet to his ear. There was the connection tone! He'd been afraid with the stadium systems all fouled up, he wouldn't be able to get a line at all.

First things first. Matt punched in the area code for the East side of Manhattan, then Leif's home phone number. 'Come on!' he muttered as electronic noises bleeped in his ear. Then the connection was made – but no one was home.

'Your call cannot be answered at this time,' a pleasant-sounding female voice purred in Matt's ear. It was the Andersons' computer system, offering him a choice of voicemail options.

Matt cut the connection, waited for the tone, and began dialing again. This time the number was shorter – the New York municipal area code plus 911.

'Emergency services,' a computerized voice came on.

'Medical emergency,' Matt said, trying to keep his words clear. He gave Matt's address and apartment number. 'Victim is alone and in shock – possible damage to subdural computer implant and neural injuries.'

Matt choked. Just a few minutes ago, he'd been joking with Leif about blowing brain cells on useless information. If whatever happened here had caused serious damage, Leif might actually have lost brain cells.

Leif hadn't moved or spoken. His holographic image became fuzzy, then faded away. Matt stared in worry.

A real voice replaced the computer interface, asking for more information. Matt tried to answer the questions, and added a fact that might hurry any rescue. 'Leif is a member of the Net Force Explorers, and so am I.' Matt then rattled off his Net Force Explorers ID number, and the number for his wallet-phone.

At least that will get some help for Leif, he thought, cutting the connection to New York. Then Matt punched in the local emergency code. There were probably hundreds of people calling in this weird virtual attack to the Baltimore police. *But one more won't hurt,* Matt thought. *Maybe this will be the call that convinces the local cops that this isn't just some sort of huge prank.*

Matt found himself again making a report to a computerized voicemail system. *Sure*, he thought, *Emergency Services must be getting flooded with calls.* He kept his story short and to the point, mentioned the Net Force Explorers, and cut the connection.

What had he missed while he'd been trying to get help?

The Gruesome Foursome still stood at the top of the bleachers, hosing the field and the seats with their tommy guns. Matt got a queasy feeling as a make-believe bullet passed through his arm, but it seemed that the virtual attack could only harm virtual spectators tied into the stadium's simulation system.

Armored figures suddenly appeared in the emptied bleachers.

Police spotters, Matt figured, popping up in holographic form to get a look at what was going on.

Hadn't they been warned about the holographic bullets? Maybe they thought their virtual armour could handle it . . . but they were wrong.

Several police observers went down, then they all shimmered and disappeared.

Matt could hear sirens converging on the stadium, and police copters appeared overhead.

The tall gangster's laughter resounded across the nearly empty ballfield. He aimed his virtual tommy gun into the sky, but the holographic bullets didn't harm real live police equipment.

'All right, people,' the pin-striped gunman's voice blared through the PA system. 'Show's over.'

His laughter, and the racheting roar of the machine guns, cut off as if a knife had sliced through the air.

Most of the people around Matt crouched or lay behind the flimsy safety of the bleachers. But Matt Hunter stood, glaring at the oddly dressed foursome who had caused so much devastation in a few short minutes.

Then the intruders were gone, without so much as a flash or shadow to mark their going.

Whoever they are, Matt thought, they have an excellent system behind them. Talk about your clean getaways . . .

Chapter 2

As a strong contingent of Baltimore police entered the stadium, Matt's wallet-phone rang. Even though the connection was staticky, Matt recognized the voice on the other end. It was Captain James Winters, the Net Force public affairs liaison. But Winters was much more than a glorified public-relations officer. He'd come up with the idea of the Net Force Explorers – and in the captain's mind, they were his troops, just as much as the Marines he'd commanded in the last Balkan blow-up.

'The local police contacted us as soon as they realized the Net was involved,' he said. 'And I hopped in a chopper as soon as I heard some of my people were involved.'

Matt grinned into the receiver. That was the captain all over – the Net Force Explorers were 'his people.'

'I want you and the others to hold yourselves in readiness to cooperate with the Baltimore police. They'll be glad to have an account of this incident from some trained observers.'

That was the captain all over, too, Matt thought. He expects the best effort from his people.

'Yes, sir,' he spoke into the phone.

'I expect to be landing in a couple of minutes. We'll rendezvous at whatever police precinct you'll be giving your statements.'

'I'll pass the word, sir.'

'Good. Winters out.'

The connection cut off. Matt passed along what the captain had said. Even as he was explaining their orders, the phone rang again.

Lucky I didn't switch configurations, he thought.

'Matthew Hunter?' an official-sounding voice crackled in his ear. 'I'm Sergeant Den Burgess, Baltimore P.D. We've been informed that you're with a contingent of Net Force Explorers here in the stadium. Could you please indicate where you are?'

'We're still in the bleachers.' Matt put a hand over his phone's pickup and turned to his remaining buddies. 'Let's get up on our seats and wave our arms.'

He got back on the phone. 'Sergeant? If you can spot a small group standing on their seats and waving, you'll have found us.'

'Got you,' the voice in his ear said. 'Expect me in a couple of minutes.' Again, the connection cut off. Matt replaced his wallet.

The police had mainly been working to clear away the crowd and trying to identify the injured holoforms still in the stadium. Now a small contingent of uniformed officers made their way through the bleachers to Matt and his friends. In the lead was a tall, black, competent-looking man with sergeant's stripes on his short-sleeved shirt. 'I'm Burgess,' he said. 'Which of you is Hunter?'

'I am,' Matt said, stepping forward.

'Looks like your group came through all right.'

Matt shook his head. 'Several of us were here in holoform. One got hit by a virtual bullet.'

Burgess looked around in concern.' Is he—?'

'I hope he's all right,' Matt said with a stab of worry. 'He's in New York. I called Emergency Services there – it was the best I could do. Everybody else in our group cut out safely.' He glanced at the sergeant. 'I've never seen anything like this happen before.'

Burgess simply shook his head. 'Neither have I, son. Neither have I.'

The sergeant took Matt and his friends to the nearest police precinct, where they each gave a statement, describing what happened as best they could. Matt had actually missed a lot of the action while he'd been trying to take care of Leif. Sergeant Burgess nodded at the description of the shock symptoms. 'That's what happened to everyone in virtual who got hit,' he said.

'I've heard that implant shock could happen to people,' Matt said. 'But I thought it only occurred in small-scale, intense sims, where you begin to lose track of what's real and what's virtual.'

'Belief plays a larger factor in virtual injuries than many people realize,' a familiar voice said.

Matt turned to see Captain Winters step up to the sergeant's desk. He held out his Net Force ID to Burgess. 'I've been upstairs in the operations center you folks have set up. We'll be coptering in additional tech and medical people.'

Burgess looked relieved. 'We can use all the help we can get.'

'Are you finished with my people here?'

'Yes, sir,' the sergeant replied. 'At least we have a pretty clear idea of what went down.' He shrugged. 'Whether we can catch whoever was responsible . . .'

Winters nodded. 'That'll be a headache for all of us.' He beckoned Matt along. 'They gave me an office upstairs.' A sour expression crossed his face. 'Not that there's much I'll be able to do here.'

'I still don't understand how it ever happened, Captain,' Matt said. 'With large-scale sims, aren't there supposed to be safety interlocks to turn off the system before people get injured?'

'There are supposed to be,' Winters admitted grimly. 'But it seems some unsung genius has managed a programming miracle that hoodwinks the safety coding. The only bright side so far is that it's not being used by terrorists or criminals.'

Matt halted, staring, as they climbed the stairs. 'You don't think what happened this afternoon was criminal?'

'Oh, no,' Winter said, still climbing. 'This was big-time law-breaking. It just wasn't done by career criminals. It was done by kids.'

'Kids?' Matt echoed.

'Teenagers,' the captain went on. 'Four of them. They've been trashing veeyars all around the Washington, D.C. area. Talking over systems remotely, wrecking whatever setups they're running, business or entertainment, blowing the computers out – and injuring whoever happens to be hooked in at the time. The victims ended up in shock, like Leif Anderson.'

Winters paused. 'By the way, I checked with Emergency

Services in New York. Leif is in stable condition – thanks to your quick response.'

Matt straightened as if a weight had come off his shoulders. 'I'm glad to hear that,' he said. 'But how does this gang get in and out?'

The captain shook his head. 'We don't really know. By the time they're finished with a system, it's pretty well blown out. We think that today's little exhibition was a test to see if they could ramshackle a big system.' He stalked down a hallway. 'If so, they were successful. Most of the memory of the Camden Yards system was slagged.'

'Even so, there were HoloNet crews there to broadcast the game,' Matt said. 'They must have gotten images of those people.'

'Oh, they did,' Winters growled as he opened an office door. Holograms of four heads floated in the air over the systems desk.

Matt recognized them all. 'That one – the round face with the big ears – that's the guy who did all the talking – the tall one.'

'It took us a little time, but we finally got a criminal records match,' Winters said.

'Great!'

The captain shook his head. 'The record was a flatfilm photo from almost a hundred years ago – 1934. That face belonged to John Dillinger.'

'Proxies,' Matt said in disgust. Sometimes people used other faces – even bodies – in virtual reality. When the technology had first been developed, proxies had been a fad. People had designed all sorts of strange creatures to represent themselves on the Net. But weirdness just hadn't cut it as the Net became more of a business workplace. The fad passed, and proxies were generally only used in personal veeyars, games, and historical simulations.

Matt had heard that some people used improved versions of themselves in virtual business meetings. And holo stars sometimes had their appearances tweaked in their shows. But nobody appeared in proxy form in public – especially as an open-air hologram!

'These people must be weird – no, eccentric,' he corrected himself. 'Rich people are eccentric, and they'd have to have lots of money to pull off what they did. Not to mention being computer geniuses.'

'They've certainly got a warped sense of humor. It took us a little longer to identify this face.' Winters pointed to a set of mustached features with a receding chin. 'That's Dr Crippen. Executed in 1910 for a sensational murder in Britain.'

He gestured towards the remaining faces. 'These two aren't even criminals at all.'

Matt stared at the laughing, lean features of a dark-haired man and the smiling, heart-shaped young woman's face. 'Who are they?'

'Actors. Warren Beatty and Faye Dunaway, circa 1967 – the year they did a gangster flatfilm called *Bonnie and Clyde*.'

Matt couldn't help himself. He chuckled.

'Sure,' Winters said angrily. 'They're just kids, kidding around. But they've hurt a lot of people. And these pranks of theirs keep escalating.'

The smile disappeared from Matt's face. 'Have you got any sort of line on them?'

The captain shook his head. 'We've had our best online

decoys out on the Net – and so far, we've gotten zilch.'

Matt examined the four false faces in front of him. 'Even the best adult operator can't impersonate a teenager perfectly,' he said. 'To catch these kids, you're going to need a kid.'

He tapped his chest. 'And I think I'm that kid.'

The next morning was a Monday, the beginning of the school week, Usually Matt had to drag himself out of bed. But today he was up, showered, dressed and finished with breakfast in lots of time for a slow walk to the bus stop. He was still turning over plans in his mind. Matt went to Bradford Academy, one of the most prestigious high schools in the Washington area. He'd gotten into the academy on a scholarship – but most of the students were bright, rich kids. If the Virtual Vandals didn't actually go to Bradford, Matt was willing to bet that somebody on campus probably knew them.

Matt flagged down the approaching autobus, climbed aboard, and swiped his Universal Credit Card past the computer system that ran the vehicle.

'Destination, please?' the operating computer asked.

Matt gave the nearest cross streets to Bradford Academy, sat down, and continued to worry at the problem he'd set for himself.

He'd have to find a way into the elite social clique at school – the Leets, Big Men (and Women) on campus, the ones who always got elected to the student government and ran the dances. Matt knew some of these kids – the smarter ones – from classes. He ran down that list. Could any of those kids have hidden behind the gun-toting proxies he'd seen yesterday? It seemed hard to believe.

But there were lots of other rich kids at Bradford, kids with enough money to afford the absolute best in computer equipment – and who were bored enough to go looking for a few sick thrills.

The bus pulled up at Matt's stop, announcing the streets. Matt got off and walked the couple of blocks to the Bradford campus. The parking lot was already filling with flashy, expensive cars – another set of toys that the rich kids who went here could afford.

Andy Moore leaned against the wall at the side entrance, trying to catch the feeble rays of sunshine. The weather had changed overnight, and the morning was downright chilly. Matt grinned when he saw how red his friend's face was. Andy *had* gotten a sunburn yesterday.

'I don't know why we're here,' Andy grumpily greeted Matt as he came up.

'Compulsory Education Act of 2009,' Matt replied, remembering his Civics homework. 'We've got to stay in school until we're at least eighteen.'

'It's a plot,' Andy said darkly. 'They could just as easily broadcast classes through the Net. I could be sitting up in bed now in my underwear, eating kelp-tarts and just preparing for the day—'

'If this is a two-way connection, that would probably be against the Cruelty to Teachers Act of 2010.'

Andy shrugged. 'Maybe.' Then he gave Matt a suspicious look. 'Hey! I don't remember any Cruelty to Teachers Act.'

'So I made it up,' Matt replied. 'You're probably right that sending us off to school is a giant baby-sitting scheme, so the folks who go to work will know their kids are being supervised—'

'And the ones who work at home will have the kids out of their hair,' Andy finished.

'I think we learn something besides Math, English, and Social Studies,' Matt said. 'School throws us in with different people, and we have to learn to get along with them. Otherwise all we'd be good for is veeyars and interfacing with the computers in autobuses.'

Andy laughed. 'Hey, at least someday I hope to be able to afford an auto*car*.'

The school doors opened, and Matt, Andy, and the other kids who'd been gathering hurried down the halls to the classroom they used for Prep Period. Matt logged on to one of the desk computers, giving his student ID number, automatically signifying his attendance and calling up the day's schedule.

Good, he thought. No surprise lecturers. As a respected school in the Washington area, Bradford attracted visitors from around the world – scholars who knew the academic staff, educators examining the workings of the school, even famous alumni. But today looked pretty straightforward – except for the request to meet with his history teacher after classes.

Matt wasn't worried about that – he liked Dr Fairlie and got along well in his class. Besides, he had other concerns right now.

Powering down his desk unit, he turned to the kids sitting around him. Andy was already talking up the incident in Baltimore.

'Hey, I was there!' Andy was telling his audience. 'It was pretty bugged up! You know Leif Anderson? He was there in virtual and got hit by one of those idiots!'

'I heard it was just a bunch of kids fooling around on the Net,' Matt said.

'If that's the way they fool around, I'd hate to see them get serious,' Lois Kearny said.

'Yeah,' Manuel Oliva added. 'This isn't like programming all the toilets in the school to flush together.' The year before they'd started at Bradford, some unknown genius had managed that trick, and moved into legend. The school authorities had never found the culprit – officially. But a huge anonymous donation had been made, probably by the kid's parents, to pay for flood damage and plumbing repairs.

'Anybody hear about anyone messing around on the Net?" Matt asked casually.

The answers were disappointing, all little stuff – like the person trying to send a love note mistakenly e-mailing it to everyone in the school.

'I hear somebody hacked a way into the commercial entertainment sims,' Mannie Oliva said.

'Pay-per-adventure,' Lois sneered, not very impressed.

'These are the special – *adult* – ones,' Mannie went on.

'Sounds like some computer geek in search of a life,' Andy hooted.

'And looking in all the wrong places,' Matt agreed.

The mysteries of schoolwork took over for the rest of the day. But Matt's investigation got an unexpected boost from Dr Fairlie. When Matt arrived at his history teacher's last-period classroom, he found a classmate waiting at the door. Sandy Braxton was one of the 'Leets.'

Dr Fairlie beckoned them in after his students came bursting out of the door. 'You know that an important part of your American history grade comes from the research project. I'm assigning the pair of you to work as a team. You both have the same topic – the Battle of Gettysburg.'

'I've been doing some research about Pickett's Charge,' Sandy said anxiously. 'The Confederate general who broke the Union line was attacking troops led by his former best friend.'

'An interesting start, Mr Braxton,' Dr Fairlie said. 'Unfortunately, your reports are more known for their flashy computer special effects than for their clear content.'

The teacher glanced at Matt. 'Mr Braxton is not a writer. Amazingly, he has reached his third year here at Bradford without being able to organize his thoughts into a coherent narrative.'

Matt knew why. Sandy Braxton probably felt he didn't *need* to organize his thoughts. When he got out of school, he could hire any organization experts he needed to help run the family business – which, as far as Matt could see, involved owning about half of Virginia.

The teacher went on. 'Your reports, Mr Hunter, are models of clarity. Perhaps you can give Mr Braxton some useful pointers.'

Frankly, Matt didn't know what – or if – he could teach Sandy Braxton. But Sandy could get Matt into the Leets, the group he wanted to check out.

He stuck out his hand and said, 'Let's get to work, partner.'

Chapter 3

Matt headed straight for his room when he arrived home. He tossed a two-inch-square datascrip onto his desk. Its memory matrix held gigabytes of information – Sandy Braxton's info dump on the two Civil War generals, Hancock and Armistead. The clatter seemed louder than usual in the empty house. Dad had a teachers' meeting, and Mom wouldn't get home from her job at the Department of Defense for at least another hour and a half.

There was lots of time for Matt to do what he intended and then get to his homework.

He sank into the computer-link chair in front of his desk, leaning back against the headrest. For an instant, there was a sort of buzzing in his ears as the receptors in the chair tuned into the circuitry implanted under Matt's skin. The desk faded from in front of Matt's eyes as he entered his own personal veeyar, the operating system for his personal computer.

Matt drifted crosslegged in the midst of a starry sky. In front of him floated a marble slab, decorated with small glowing objects – icons representing various programs in the computer.

Stretching out a finger, Matt touched an inch-tall, neon blue telephone and thought of Leif Anderson's telecom number. A second later, he felt the twinge of a connection. Matt composed a mental message. *Leif, it's Matt. Would you mind a virtual visit?*

Letters of flame appeared in the air. *Come on up!*

Matt moved from the tiny telephone and picked up a little gold thunderbolt, his interconnect icon. He thought again of Leif's number, and the universe went slightly out of focus and he transferred to the Net.

Now Matt seemed to be flying through a vast city of light. Soaring skyscrapers in single blazing colors marked major corporate Web nodes. Other virtual buildings were gray, with each window shining a different color – small-business and individual e-mail sites. Yet other constructs floated in the coal-black sky. Matt flew past them at blurring speed, since his destination was already set.

He flashed on through the virtual landscape until he came to a glowing silver building, then arrowed towards an entire floor of red-hued windows – the family suite of the Anderson family.

The moment he reached the virtual window, Matt blinked – and found himself standing in Leif's room.

Matt blinked again. This was unexpected. He assumed he'd land in Leif's personal veeyar, not out in the real world in holoform. Matt shook his head. 'I didn't know you had your room hooked up for full holo projection.'

'Oh, it's the hot thing to do, if your folks have enough money.' Leif would have been better off if he could have hidden behind a virtual mask. His skin was pale, and his face seemed twisted in pain even though he sat in a large, comfortable chair. He was wearing pajamas and a robe.

'Still recovering from that hit, huh?'

Leif nodded – and winced. 'Ever been caught in veeyar when a program suddenly crashed?'

'Who hasn't? Usually you wind up with a killer headache.'

'Multiply that by about a hundred, and you'll have an idea of how I feel. Gah! It even hurts to listen to myself talk.'

Leif sighed, carefully letting his head rest back against the chair. 'My implant is okay, and the doctors say there's no nerve damage, just . . . sensitivity.' His lips crooked in a half-smile. 'No veeyar until the neurons calm down. And out here in regular reality, well, my folks are delighted. No loud music, no action holos with sirens, car chases, and explosions . . . in other words, no fun for a while.'

He sent a sharp look Matt's way. 'There hasn't been much on the HoloNet about what went down in Camden Yards. I can't believe the cops don't have a clue. Has Net Force clamped down on it? What was it all about? Terrorists?'

'It was kids,' Matt said. 'The cops – and Net Force – have no idea who they are.'

He went on to explain what Captain Winters had told him.

Leif frowned. 'What sort of sickos would even consider shooting down a field full of hologram baseball players?' Then he answered his own question. 'Spoiled, *rich*, sick kids, messing people up for fun – no profit.'

'Maybe it was people who hate baseball,' Matt suggested.

'You mean the sorts of geekoids who never got chosen to

play on a team?' Leif leaned forward in his chair. 'We're looking at money and brains here. And if it's kids with money in the D.C. area, I should know them – or know people who know them.'

Leif sank back, eyes shut, sighing. 'You know, I'd be just the right person to track down these virtual vandals – if I could get on the Net.'

He darted another look at Matt. '*You're* after them, aren't you?'

Matt nodded. 'I'm trying, but I could use some help.'

'Bet you could.' Leif was still frowning, but now he was frowning in thought. 'It will mean dealing with a different crowd than you're used to, even going to Rich Kids' Prep.'

Matt laughed. 'What's that old saying? "The rich are different?" '

But Leif didn't join his laughter. 'They're only interested in who's got more money or social clout. That's why they like diplomats – usually they've got money *and* clout. Pull some stupid prank, and the State Department will hush it up.'

'You think that some of the vandals may be diplomats' kids?' Matt asked.

'It's possible,' Leif said. 'Nothing like a little diplomatic immunity to make a person completely irresponsible.' He looked at Matt. 'But that doesn't help you get in with them. Rich kids are always ready to use you—'

Matt suddenly thought of Sandy Bradford and the 'help' he'd be getting.

'Or you could interest them – which is just using you in a different way – for entertainment.'

'Hey, you're a rich kid, too,' Matt said. 'You're dumping on your own sort of people pretty hard.'

'I've met my share of snobs and users,' Leif said curtly. 'I'm familiar with them. And to use another old saying, "Familiarity breeds contempt." '

He thought for another moment, then said, 'Computer! Identify for voice commands.'

'Voice identified as Leif Anderson,' the computer's response was quiet, yet it seemed to fill the room.

'File transfer. Proxy, entree, Maxim dot com. Iconize.' Leif turned to Matt. 'Hand out, buddy.'

As Matt stretched out his holoform hand, a small chess piece popped into existence on his palm. It was a pawn, maybe an inch tall, made of swirling red fire.

'That's a program you'll be able to take back with you through the Net,' Leif said. 'Run it through your computer, and you'll have the coordinates and a password for a very special Web-node – a virtual chat room.'

'Oh, great,' Matt muttered.

'I said it was special,' Leif said. 'It's a chat room for the young, rich, and restless. Nobody shows up in his or her real face. Everyone uses proxies – the wilder, the better.' He paused for a second. 'That's the rest of the program. I developed a new proxy for myself, something to catch the attention of the people who hang out there.'

Matt stared at his friend. 'You go to this chat room?'

Leif laughed, but there wasn't a trace of humor in his voice. 'Oh, yeah. I like to hang out with the rich kids, too. Even if it means I have to interest and entertain them.'

After returning home through the Net, Matt finished his

classwork, then had dinner. Only then did he reconnect to his computer and reach for the swirling red pawn. When the proxy program was activated, Matt called up a virtual mirror to check himself out.

Was this some sort of joke? Leif's program had transformed him into an animated stick figure – a sort of quick freehand figure with tiny dots for eyes and a line for a mouth. Even as Matt watched, the figure began turning red – from embarrassment.

Had Leif really intended to enter that chat room as a walking doodle?

Then Matt thought for a moment. The stick-figure *would* offer him a perfect disguise. And if Leif was right, it would get him noticed. Matt decided to give it a try. So what if he wound up feeling like an idiot? He could always disconnect, and nobody would even know that Matt Hunter had been there.

Matt looked down and saw he wasn't red anymore. He reached out with one stick-figure hand for his gold thunderbolt. His other hand grasped the red pawn with the destination and password.

Let's go, he thought.

Matt swirled wildly across the neon cityscape of the Net, heading into areas he'd never explored before. The virtual constructions here were spread out more widely – surrounded by security zones, Matt suddenly realized. The developers had also fooled around more in designing them. Matt flashed past what looked like a neon graveyard, a glowing replica of Dracula's castle, and finally came to a halt at a set of red-and-gold gates.

A hulking, faceless figure confronted him. Matt quickly

flashed the password he'd been given. He had no desire to find out what that glaring creature of light did to intruders.

The glowing gatekeeper flashed, transforming into a tall, thin man in an old-fashioned tuxedo – the image of a headwaiter at a super-expensive restaurant.

'Please to follow me, sir or madam.' The waiter spoke with an accent – French, Matt realized.

He stepped through the gateway, to find himself in a setting of the sort he'd only seen in holos. Matt stood in a large hall, decorated in the style of the nineties – the 1890s. Everything seemed to be red or gold – red satin wallpaper, plush red velvet drapes and chairs. Brassy gold columns held up a ceiling that seemed to be hammered gold leaf. Private balconies were trimmed with gold. Even the flame of the old-fashioned gaslights had a golden glow.

Part of the hall was set up as a restaurant, with black-clad waiters zooming among the tables. Another part was a casino, full of games of chance. A small orchestra played ancient music for an almost empty dance floor.

But most of the huge space was just an expanse of red-and-gold rug, where figures of all sorts walked along, sometimes passing, sometimes speaking to one another.

Matt found himself staring. Off to one side was a giant red-and-gold robot whose head almost scraped the ceiling fifty feet above. People stood in his (its?) outstretched palm, chatting. A superhero swaggered by, every muscle showing in his skintight uniform. Behind him hopped a perfectly natural-looking frog – except if this frog stood up, it would be a good six feet tall.

Another figure passed by – Matt recognized it as a cartoon character he'd followed on Saturday mornings. Beyond was something even weirder – a human skull haloed in fire, floating in midair at about eye level.

Well, Matt thought, guess I don't have to worry about fitting in.

'First time at Maxim's?' a girl's voice asked from behind him.

He turned to find a young blond woman who looked, well, normal – except for the fact that she was very beautiful.

'Um . . . yeah,' Matt admitted.

'You're turning red!' she said, laughing. 'I love it!'

'I think it's a fault in the program,' Matt said in embarrassment.

'No, it's great,' the girl insisted. 'What's your proxy name?'

'I don't—' Matt began.

'We'll call you . . . Mr Sticks,' the girl said. 'I'm CeeCee, by the way.'

'Nice to meet you, CeeCee.' Matt knew he was staring at her, but this woman looked familiar. Then it hit him. She was a soap star on the HoloNet, Courtney Vance!

Or rather, he warned himself, she's the *image* of Courtney Vance. Who knows who's behind the mask?

'From the way you don't seem very impressed by all this, I'd guess you come here pretty often,' Matt said.

CeeCee laughed, twirling her long blond hair around one of her perfectly manicured fingers. 'You mean I don't bother getting dressed for it?'

Compared to the elaborate get-ups on most of the proxies

in Maxim's, her clothes were refreshingly down-to-earth – jeans and a loose sweater.

Then Matt found himself staring again. He'd have sworn that CeeCee's sweater was purple. Now it seemed to be dark blue. No, light blue, which was now shifting into green. 'Do your clothes go all the way through the spectrum?' he asked.

The girl laughed again. 'It's a design for a real sweater. Something to do with microfiber optics and a phased discharge . . .'

'What happens when the battery runs out?' Matt asked.

CeeCee glanced at him. 'I dunno,' she confessed. 'Maybe it goes transparent!'

'Good idea if you should just wear it in virtual, then,' Matt said. 'The worst that can happen is that you'll be rated Holo-R.'

'Nah, this is just a one-time thing, Mr Sticks,' CeeCee replied. 'You keep turning up in the same proxy, and people begin to guess who you are.' She nodded to a big, buff barbarian dressed in a wolfskin. 'That's Walton Wheatley.'

'Walt the Weed?' Matt burst out. The guy had gotten the nickname because he was so tall and skinny.

'You know Walt?' CeeCee said. 'Do you go to Bradford, too?'

You're supposed to be here finding out about these people, Matt silently scolded himself. *Not giving* them *information.*

'Got me,' he had to admit.

'There are lots of kids from Bradford here,' CeeCee said. 'Although they all want you to think they're in college – or even older.' Scowling, she hooked a thumb at the tall, red-haired woman with bold blue eyes and nothing much on. Oddly, most of the proxies seemed to be avoiding her. 'She'll *tell* you she works at her family's brokerage, but she's really in my class. That's Pat Twonky.'

Besides suffering from a comical name, Pat was a big lump of a girl with a sullen personality. Now Matt understood why people were staying away.

He also realized that CeeCee had just told him that *she* went to Bradford.

'I guess I should thank you for the warning,' Matt told her. 'But ripping away people's masks is a dangerous hobby. Now you've got me thinking about *you*. Do I just go with the blond and beautiful image I see here, or should I try to look behind it? Maybe you're just a wannabe blond – actually you've got stringy, mousy-brown hair.'

'Yikes!' CeeCee exclaimed. A couple of strands of hair wrapped around her finger came loose. Unconsciously, her fingers tied them into a little bow. 'What a nasty thing to say!'

'Or maybe you're a computer geekette, who's just here to see how the other half lives.'

'More like the other ten percent,' CeeCee corrected. 'Is that why you're here?'

Matt ignored the dig. 'Suppose,' he went on, 'you don't exist at all! Maybe you're a computer sim, set up to clue in newcomers to Maxim's.'

CeeCee had to clamp her lips together, but they curved enchantingly upward. Matt could barely hear her laughter. 'You're terrible,' she accused. 'And paranoid, if you're worrying about flirting with a sim.'

'Helps keep me real,' Matt replied. 'What else can I do when I meet someone who looks perfect no matter what color her sweater is?'

You're letting yourself get distracted, a little voice warned in the back of his head. He was saying things he'd normally never say to a girl. But, working from behind his proxy, it was just so easy to go with the flow, to play the game.

Beyond CeeCee's smiling face, a new figure swam into existence – another visitor arriving at Maxim's. The newcomer was a tall female figure, completely surrounded in a cloud of veils.

The veiled woman started past them, then suddenly whipped round to confront CeeCee. 'Hey!' an angry voice demanded. 'I thought players here were supposed to come as proxies, not copies.'

'The house rules say come as you want,' CeeCee answered sulkily.

'Probably some pimply-faced little high-school twit who wonders what it's like to be "*pretty*." ' Matt couldn't believe how much scorn the stranger put into that one word. 'It's not enough to start work before the sun rises, spend most of your free time learning lines, and have little idiots copy your hairdo. But I draw the line at rich get-a-lifes stealing my face!'

Matt stared back and forth between the two young women. This had to be the real Courtney Vance – and, boy, was she in a bad mood!

CeeCee's face was red with embarrassment – and anger. 'I'd call it more borrowing for a night. And I came as Alicia Fieldston.'

That was the character Courtney portrayed, Matt remembered.

'You know,' CeeCee went on. 'The character with the improvements the studio adds, so I wouldn't look like this—' Suddenly, CeeCee's eyebrows became heavy and ragged. 'Or this . . .' Her perfect nose went a little off-center.

'Why, you little—' the real Courtney Vance growled.

But the girl in the virtual copy had heard enough. CeeCee suddenly swung, her fist catching the veiled figure in the side of the jaw.

Matt winced as he heard the impact of knuckles against flesh and bone. That had to hurt!

The real Courtney Vance vanished like a popped soap bubble.

Matt stood where he was, the thought still echoing in his brain. *That had to hurt.* CeeCee had harmed Courtney Vance with a virtual attack. CeeCee had to be one of the people he was looking for!

He turned to the girl, who was shaking out her fist.

But before Matt could speak, they were joined by a figure that towered over them both. It was roughly in the shape of a human, if humans came nine feet high and were constructed of glowing crystals. Instantly, Matt christened the intruder Mr Jewels.

The crystalline figure lumbered up to CeeCee. 'Can't leave you on your tod even for a couple of minutes, can I?'

The voice was supposed to sound like wind chimes. But anger gave it a harsh, clanging tone.

A hand clamped on CeeCee's arm. Although the finger-crystals glowed softly, Matt knew they must be hard as stone. CeeCee merely looked at Mr Jewels in silence, her face a mask of fear – and pain.

I've got to do something, Matt thought, even as he wondered how his stick-body would survive being stomped by those big, rocky feet.

But before he could move, CeeCee and her big, jeweled friend both vanished from Maxim's.

Chapter 4

Matt yawned as he rode the autobus to school the next morning. He'd spent a sleepless night going over what he'd learned from his virtual visit to Maxim's.

Not that it amounts to all that much, he thought as he walked onto the academy campus.

During prep period, he pulled Andy and David Gray aside. 'Leif got me into a rich kids' virtual hangout last night,' he reported. 'I think I may have met some of our friends from Camden Yards.'

'Which ones?' Andy immediately asked. 'John Dillinger, or the cute blond?'

'I can't be sure,' Matt admitted. 'They were in different proxies, of course. One was a guy made up of crystals – I called him Mr Jewels. The other was a girl named CeeCee. She came as Courtney Vance.'

'You mean the actress who plays the doctor on *Central Hospital*?' David asked.

'I didn't know you watched the holo-soaps,' Andy teased.

'Come on,' David defended himself. 'Her image is all over the Net.'

'It sure is.' Andy thought for a second. 'Very pretty, and very blond.'

'It might be a clue,' Matt said. 'If CeeCee is the same girl from the stadium, she likes to appear as a blond – maybe she has blond hair.'

'Or maybe she's a wannabe blond,' Andy shot back. 'I came across a dictionary of old-fashioned slang – Valley Speak, they called it. They had a couple of names for girls with blond hair – loxies, and boxies.'

Matt and David glanced at each other, baffled.

'A loxie is like Goldilocks – she gets her blond hair from Ma Nature,' Andy explained with a grin. 'Other girls got their blond hair from a box. Nowadays, they can play proxies who look the way they want to. Your CeeCee may weigh three hundred pounds and have a shaved head.'

'Got any other clues for Sherlock over here to trash?' David asked.

'The real Courtney Vance turned up,' Matt said. 'CeeCee hit her – and hurt her.'

Both of his friends stopped kidding. 'What happened then?' Andy asked.

'Then this jewel-guy came lumbering over. He complained about not being able to leave CeeCee on her tod.' Matt smiled, proud of himself. 'I tracked down that expression on the Net – it's British slang for leaving someone alone. So Mr Jewels may be British – maybe somebody from the diplomatic community.'

'Or maybe it's someone pretending to be British,' David objected. 'Have you heard about that new proxy program, Idiom Savant? It instantly translates whatever you say into a dozen other languages. The only giveaway is in the lips of the proxy. There's a slight delay between the lip movements and the sound as the program processes the translation.'

'Oh, perfect,' Matt groaned as the others laughed. 'This jewel-guy didn't have any lips at all!'

Sandy Braxton caught up with Matt that day at lunch. 'So? Have you read any of the information on that datascrip I gave you? I found a big file about how many Civil War generals were officers together in the Mexican War. Hancock and Armistead both served together in Winfield Scott's army. Lots of the officers who were in Pickett's charge were also in the attack on Chapultepec Castle – including Pickett and James Longstreet.'

'That's really interesting,' Matt said nervously. With his visit to Maxim's, he hadn't even looked at the scrip. 'Maybe we can make that the opening of our report. Can you tell me some more?'

Sandy glanced over to one of the tables in the cafeteria. 'I was going to sit with some of my friends—'

Matt followed his eyes. Of course, it was a group of Leets – and there were three blond girls. 'Well, maybe we can do it between bites,' he suggested.

Sandy shrugged and led the way to the cafeteria line, where they loaded a pair of trays. Then Matt followed his new friend to the table full of Leets.

One of the girls looked ready to say something as Matt took a seat, but Sandy quickly spoke up. 'This is Matt Hunter from my history class. We're working on a project together.'

The girl muttered something to her friends. All Matt caught was, '—could've taken the geek to another table, then.' The rest was drowned out by a wave of laughter and one girl's, 'Lighten up, Tricia.'

Matt did his best to control his expression, ignoring Tricia's nasty comment, pretending to be interested as Sandy rambled on about ancient history, while forcing down cafeteria mystery glop and keeping an eye on the three blond girls. It was like juggling four things at once. He could only hope he didn't drop one.

For instance, he had to listen to enough of what Sandy was saying to say something every once in a while. And he couldn't make it obvious that he was checking the girls out. As far as he could figure, any of them could be the mysterious CeeCee.

Each girl seemed to hold her head at an angle and laugh as they joked and teased one another. And all of them, blond or brunette, twirled their hair around their fingertips as they talked. Some of the stuff they said he didn't even understand. They either had their own in-group lingo, or they were using slang that hadn't caught on yet with the rest of the mere mortals at Bradford.

'So, you going to the V.I.P.-VP at Lara Fortune's on Friday?' Tricia asked.

Apparently her slang was too advanced for one of the girls. 'The V-I-who-what?' she asked.

'V.I.P. – very important person. VP – Virtual Party,' Tricia explained with a toss of her head.

Another girl rolled her eyes. 'Krishna, but virtual parties are so . . . so *heatherish*.'

Matt got that comment. Heather was a very old-fashioned girl's name, from before the turn of the century. The girl was saying that virtual parties were pretty much past it.

When he stopped to think about it, the last one he'd been to had been for a friend's seventh birthday.

'Not this one – it's going to be red-line all the way. Her daddy shelled out big bucks for a way unbelievable locale. I know my dad blew a few zeroes for my virtual gown.'

'Gown?' the other girls chorused.

'It's gonna be drop-dead formal,' Tricia announced smugly. 'No proxies allowed – just your image and whatever someone can hack up for you.'

'I guess it will have to depend on my programmer,' one of the blonds said, twirling a lock of hair tightly around her forefinger.

'Not much time,' Tricia warned.

The other girl shrugged and grinned. 'That's what performance bonuses are for.'

Matt had to hide a grin of his own. Some poor programmer was in for a busy week. He forced himself back to Sandy, who was finally running down on his verbal data dump.

'It's interesting stuff, good for a few paragraphs maybe, but I think you're going overboard. These guys knew each other for years and years. This is just one small story.'

Sandy looked disappointed. 'But I thought—'

'We're supposed to concentrate on the Civil War, not stuff that happened almost twenty years before,' Matt said.

He tried to ignore the sneering comment from one of the girls as they got up to leave. 'A real Dexter,' she muttered – another way of calling him a nerd.

Lunch was almost over, and everyone began leaving their seats. Matt rose, too, then he suddenly froze.

'What's the matter?' Sandy asked.

Matt pulled his eyes away from one of the little trays the girls had left. Sitting on the plastic was a little bow, woven together from strands of blond hair. He'd seen CeeCee tie a little knot like that at Maxim's!

'That girl who was sitting here,' Matt said, tapping the chair in front of the tray. 'I don't think she's in any of my classes, but she looks familiar.'

'Caitlin?' Sandy shrugged. 'Maybe you saw her on holo with her dad – Senator Corrigan?' He paused for a second. 'If you're interested, well, I wouldn't say you were out of your league—'

Yes, you would, Matt said silently.

'But Cat Corrigan is sort of – high maintenance – you know?'

Caitlin Corrigan. Slur those initials together, and you got . . . CeeCee.

No, Matt thought, he didn't know much about Caitlin Corrigan. But he meant to find out.

Leif Anderson looked better when Matt came visiting him again through his computer. Although he sat in the same chair, Leif's face wasn't as pale, and he wore jeans and a sweater instead of pajamas and a robe. 'How's it going, Sherlock?' Leif asked with a grin.

'I may have a suspect from the Leets at school,' Matt reported. 'Caitlin Corrigan.'

Leif's eyebrows shot up. 'Whoa! The senator's daughter?'

'What I need to know is how to get next to her.'

Leif didn't seem to find that funny. He sat straight up in his chair, his lips going thin. 'So you thought you'd check in with your old pal Leif to get a few lessons in social climbing?'

Matt was surprised at the sharp response. 'I – I just thought that you knew these people.'

'That doesn't necessarily mean that I like them,' Leif shot back, then rubbed his forehead. 'I'm still feeling crummy,' he confessed. 'You've been in touch with me. So have David, and Andy, and most of the Net Force Explorers I know. A couple of pals here in New York have called to see how I was doing. But most of my rich so-called friends haven't even bothered to punch in my number.'

'That sounds pretty cold,' Matt said.

'As far as those kids are concerned, I *am* a social climber.' Leif grimaced. 'My father is a self-made man – that makes us what these folks call "new money." Cat Corrigan's great-grandfather collected the family loot that paid for her grandfather's political career. Her dad's, too.'

'So what are you saying? She's way out of my league?'

'I'm saying you can't get in with that group – you can't compete with their money.' Leif raised a finger. 'But most of them, all they've *got* is money. When you're rich, you don't need brains, or hard work, or the other things we think are so necessary for success.'

All of a sudden, Matt found himself thinking of Sandy Braxton. 'I think I know what you mean,' he said.

'Skill and sneakiness can beat money any day,' Leif told him. 'It's how I got in with these people. You've just got to be outrageous.'

Matt nodded. 'Like that crazy stick-figure proxy of yours.'

Leif nodded. 'Exactly. How can you catch her attention, and make her want more?'

A faint smile came over Matt's face. 'I'm beginning to get an idea, but I'm going to need your help. We've only got a couple of days to get ready.'

I guess Tricia was right, Matt thought as he synced in to Lara Fortune's virtual party. The locale was red-lined all the way – and it had cost Papa Fortune a lot of money. He seemed to be standing on the inside wall of a clear plastic disk orbiting high over the Earth. The planet looked like a grotesquely inflated moon looming over them. Fluffy white clouds covered blue oceans and brownish-green land masses. Matt squinted, trying to figure out where they were. He spotted the distinctively hooked arm of Cape Cod and grinned. Of course. They were in orbit over Washington.

The illusion was perfect in every way. A girl peering through one of several telescopes by the wall suddenly squealed, 'There's my yard! And my mom is waving at me.' The detail work in this sim had cost a fortune. Music blared overhead, and Matt looked up to find that some people had abandoned the disk-floor to float and dance in microgravity. Not the nasty-mouthed Tricia, of course. She stood in her expensive gown, clinging to the edge of a table.

Cat Corrigan must have had better spies. She wore a silver-blue silky jumpsuit that was perfectly suited for zero-g dancing. Laughing, the blond girl spun in midair. Then she spotted Matt.

Or, rather, she spotted the stick-figure proxy Matt had worn to the party. Caitlin bounced through the other dancers in a mad scramble, climbed down to where Matt stood, and goggled at him. 'What are *you* doing here?' she hissed.

'Just checking out a suspicion, CeeCee,' Matt replied

lazily. 'Or should I call you Cat? I've been trying to track you down ever since I saw you hit that girl at Maxim's. You've got a couple of virtual tricks I'd love to learn.'

Caitlin continued to stare as if any words she might say would choke her. But she didn't get a chance to say anything.

At that moment another blond girl, wearing an even fancier jumpsuit, came up to them. 'I don't know how you got in, but if you had an invitation, you'd know that proxies aren't allowed.' Lara Fortune turned to Caitlin. 'Do you know him, Cat?'

'N – no,' Caitlin Corrigan gulped. Her eyes still hadn't left Matt's proxy.

'I'm terribly sorry,' Matt said. 'I'm sure I have my invitation somewhere.' He went through the motions of a man searching his pockets, which looked ridiculous on a stick figure. 'Aha!' he exclaimed, pulling something out of thin air.

It wasn't an invitation-icon, however. Matt shook out something that looked like a rubbery, black pancake.

'What is that?' Lara Fortune demanded.

Matt tossed it to her. It landed on the front of her lace and spandex jumpsuit, creating a disgusting inky smear down the front. 'It's a virtual stain. Pretty neat, huh? Or then again, maybe not.'

Lara's response to the destruction of her costume was an ear-piercing scream.

Matt stepped back. 'Maybe I should try and distract you.' This time he came out with what looked like a handful of small pebbles. He turned to a nearby table, where a complicated collection of tubes created a microgravity fountain over the punchbowl. But when he tossed his handful of pebbles in, the contents of the bowl began to bubble and send up clouds of steam. Then came a muted *ba-BOOM*! A mushroom cloud of punch rose into the air and began drifting lazily downward in the low gravity. The muffled explosion caused screams and stares.

Cat Corrigan tried to brush off the sweat, sticky drizzle that began coming down on everybody in the room. 'Yuck!' she cried as punch began soaking into her outfit and hair.

A furious Lara Fortune had already whirled off to get her parents. In a second, Matt knew, automated security would be closing in on him.

'Take it easy, Cat,' he said with a nonchalant wave. 'By the way, nice party.'

From the way Caitlin came dashing at him, Matt wondered if she were going to try tackling him to keep him there.

But all she did was yank loose one of her earrings and stuff it into his hand. 'Figure it out when you're well away from here,' she muttered in the midst of the chaos. 'Just get out – now!'

Chapter 5

Saturday morning, Matt asked some of his Net Force Explorer friends to make a virtual visit. They all hovered in Matt's personal veeyar, leaning over the floating marble slab/table, examining the earring Caitlin Corrigan had given Matt the night before.

'So, at least you wound up with a souvenir from your party-crashing,' Andy Moore said. 'You think this senator's kid likes you?'

'That's not the point,' David Gray interrupted. 'You usually can't just take off virtual bits and pieces and have them survive. This earring should have faded away when Matt cut his connection with that party. Since it didn't, we know there's more to this than meets the eye.'

Silently, Matt handed over a program icon from the collection on his marble desktop – the magnifying glass.

When David held it over the earring, tiny letters sprang into being in the air – thousands of lines of them. David fiddled with the magnifying glass, making the holographic image larger, then scrolling the lines up and down.

'So,' he said in satisfaction, 'it's a program – a communications protocol.'

'Wouldn't it have been simpler if she'd just passed on her telephone number?' Andy asked.

'Maybe,' Matt admitted. 'But these are Leets we're talking about here. Rich kids. What I'm interested in is the programming, though. You guys are more up on that than I am.' Although Matt had programmed up the virtual stain he'd used on Lara Fortune's dress, he'd depended on Andy for the punchbowl surprise. 'What can you tell me?'

Both boys began scanning through the lines of programming language. 'It's very good, if a bit flashy,' David said. 'It compresses a lot of information into such a small artifact.'

'Professional,' Andy added.

'Professional as in very good amateur, or is it the work of a paid program designer?' Matt asked.

'No way this could be homemade,' Andy said. 'There are copyright notices on some of the subroutines. This is commercial program coding – very high-end, special-designed stuff. Expensive.'

'So Caitlin couldn't have written it herself?'

Andy shot him a surprised look. 'I didn't know Caitlin Corrigan was a hacker.'

'Neither do I,' Matt said. 'That's what I'm hoping to find out. Somebody had to write the coding that let the virtual vandals take over the Camden Yards computer sim system, not to mention the programming wrinkle that lets these kids hurt people in virtual realities. Let's call him – or her – the Genius. From what you're saying, I can scratch Caitlin off my list as the brains behind the vandals. She doesn't do her own programming.'

Andy gave him a shrewd look. 'Are you sure you're not letting her off because you like her?'

Matt could feel his face growing warm as he tried to defend himself. 'I don't think so,' he said.

I hope not, he thought.

'Whether she's the Genius or not, Caitlin is my connection to the other virtual vandals,' Matt said. 'That's what I've got to keep my attention on.'

'Right.' Andy gave him a wry grin. 'Whatever you do, *don't* think about the fact that she wants to see you again.'

'I could kill that idiot,' Matt muttered as he sat in his room, facing his computer console.

Andy Moore had a nasty habit of dropping little bombs into a conversation that could go off minutes or even hours after he had gone – like that little zinger about Caitlin Corrigan.

It was now early afternoon. David and Andy had left ages ago. Mom and Dad were out taking care of errands. And Matt sat staring at his computer with sightless eyes.

Just don't think about it. The words seemed to echo in his head.

An old story he'd read as a kid came out of his memory. A man suffering from a terrible illness went to the Wise Man of the Mountain to find a cure. 'It is easily done,' the Wise Man said. 'You must go through a day without thinking of elephants.'

Of course, that didn't cure the sufferer's disease. How can people spend any period of time not thinking of something they're consciously trying to avoid? The thought keeps popping up, like a pesky toothache.

Matt sighed and settled himself in his computer-link chair. He forced himself to relax, letting the chair's receivers

51

tune into his implants. Telling the thought to go away didn't seem to be accomplishing much. Doing something was the answer.

In this case, the something would be a virtual visit to Caitlin Corrigan.

Matt opened his eyes and found himself floating in the starry twilight, facing the unsupported marble slab. In the middle was Cat's earring, right where they'd left it. Matt reached out, then suddenly pulled his hand back. Instead, he went for the glowing red pawn Leif had given him.

Glancing down, he saw he'd been reduced to a stick figure again. Only after donning the proxy disguise did Matt take up Cat's earring and the lightning-bolt teleconnection icon.

An instant later, he was flashing across the neon cityscape of the Net. Matt found himself passing several governmental constructs. *Not surprising*, he thought, *when you considered that Caitlin's dad was a senator.*

But, suddenly, before he got too deep into government territory, the communication protocol sent him veering off. This was the equivalent of a wealthy, quiet neighborhood on the edges of the government's systems. The virtual houses were large, but not quite as self-indulgent as a vampire castle or the mansion that housed Maxim's.

Matt realized his course was taking him to a modest-looking structure with a porch and pillars. It looked strangely familiar. Then Matt recognized it. He was flying toward a simplified version of Mount Vernon, George Washington's eighteenth-century plantation house.

But he wasn't headed for a door or window. Matt was flying toward a blank wall.

He found himself remembering that Cat's gang could use virtual technology to hurt people.

Nice going, Matt thought. They could crash me out right in front of Caitlin's house. After the stunts I pulled last night, who's going to believe me when I try to explain.

At the last moment, Matt jerked to a stop so sudden, it would have flung his stomach up to his throat in real life. As it was, he found himself staring at a neon-white wall.

Okay, Matt thought. Obviously I'm supposed to do something. But what?

Cat hadn't given him a password. Unless . . .

He extended the virtual hand that held Cat's earring/ doohickey. The fist sank into the wall – and so did Matt.

A moment later, he found himself in a veeyar – a perfectly flat landscape patterned like a checkerboard, vanishing off into the distance. Fluffy clouds passed overhead, and in between weird, twisted constructs floated in midair.

Interesting, Matt thought, looking around. Lots of money went into this. He recognized one of the flying constructs as a compressed version of a very expensive virtual game. But the veeyar didn't show much in the way of programming genius. Matt's own veeyar had more personally coded touches. Most important, there was one serious lack. Caitlin Corrigan was nowhere to be seen.

Matt was just about to pull out when the girl suddenly appeared. This was a Caitlin he'd never seen before. She wore shorts and a T-shirt, her blond hair was disheveled, held back by a terrycloth band, and her face was sweaty.

'I was in the gym when the beeper went off—' Caitlin began. Then she halted as she took in Matt's proxy figure. 'Well,' she said. 'You're seeing me at my worst. The least you could do is drop that stupid proxy and let me know who you are.'

'I'm touched that you didn't proxy up when you knew I was here,' Matt replied. 'But I had to work to track you down, and it's only fair that you work a little to find me.'

'Who are you?' Cat burst out. 'Why are you popping up around me?'

'I'm interested in you . . . and your friends . . . and what the four of you did in Camden Yards.'

Caitlin's face went white. 'I – I don't know what you're talking about,' she stammered.

'Caitlin, Caitlin, you might like to proxy up as actresses, but you're no actress yourself. Your face just gave you away.'

Caitlin bit her lip, and Matt went on. 'Hey, I'm not here to arrest you. I'm a kid, not a cop. You saw what I could do at Lara's party. But what you guys can do – I'm way impressed. I'd like to meet the masters, that's all.'

Cat Corrigan looked at him in silence for a long moment. Then she gave a jerky nod. 'All right. I'll see what I can do. Hang here. I've got to talk to the others first.'

She vanished, leaving Matt alone in her big, rich kids' playground. He walked around, playing tourist, checking out the floating constructs. They were all various expensive programs, big programs, cleverly compressed for instant use.

Biggest bunch of icons I ever saw, Matt thought, a little disappointed. The whole veeyar was just a standard setup, pricey, but lacking any sense of personal involvement. Cat hadn't tried to customize it to her own personality at all.

She must be almost computer-illiterate, Matt thought. How did she get involved with the virtual vandals at all?

He became sharply aware that time was passing. What was Caitlin doing? Had she decided to freshen up before contacting her friends? Or maybe she'd bailed out to warn them, and they were trying to decide what to do with him. Could they be trying to trace his path back through the Net? Maybe they were working to trap him in here!

Matt was on the verge of breaking contact when Caitlin returned to the veeyar. She was trying to clamp a blank expression on her face, but Matt could tell she was unhappy.

'They'll talk to you, but not here.' Cat held out an icon in her hand – a little black skull.

Great, Matt thought. But he'd come too far to be scared off now. Silently, he reached out to take Caitlin's hand.

It was a short hop through the Net, quick and confusing. That was probably done on purpose, Matt figured, to make it harder for me to track them down.

They lurched wildly through several Net sites, then came to rest in an empty virtual room. The walls were so white they almost hurt Matt's eyes.

But he wasn't paying any attention to the walls.

He was busy checking out the three proxies who stood waiting for them. They were a weird collection. The hulking, gleaming Mr Jewels was there. So was the six-foot frog. They were accompanied by a figure that looked like an animated drawing of a cowboy.

'Mr Dillinger, Mr Beatty, and Dr Crippen, I presume,' Matt said, determined not to show any fear.

'Yuh know, podnuh, you been stickin' your nose in places you really shouldn't have oughta,' the cowboy said in the thickest Wild West accent Matt had ever heard. 'Somebody ought have learned you that's dangerous.'

Right then, Matt noticed that there was the barest hesitation between the cowboy's words and the movements of his lips.

But there was no slowness at all as the cowboy whipped out his cartoon pistol and pointed it at Matt's head.

'I aim to give you a *good* lesson,' the cowboy said.

Chapter 6

Matt had seen manholes that were smaller than the muzzle of the cartoon pistol in front of his face.

'Okay, Tex, you've got my attention,' he said, still determined not to give in to the fear spurting along his nerves.

These people know how to hand out pain in virtual situations, a terrified little voice chattered in the back of his head. What would it feel like to get hit by a bullet from that hand-cannon?

The giant frog suddenly changed shape, too, transforming into a rakish-looking young nobleman dressed in the fashion of hundreds of years ago. Long black hair was pulled back in a ponytail, skintight pale leather trousers covered his legs. He wore a ruffled silk shirt – and the smile on his handsome features was as razor-sharp as the yardlong sword he aimed at Matt's throat.

And, of course, Mr Jewels didn't need a weapon. He just loomed behind the other two, clenching gleaming fists, each as large as Matt's head.

'I really have to hand it to you guys,' he told the threatening threesome – and the worried-looking girl. 'You're good ... *really* good. At first, I couldn't believe what I was hearing when I heard the first reports about what happened in Baltimore. Then I checked out every frame of the holo-imagery shot at the game, and ran a Net search to see if anything else like this had ever happened in the Washington area.'

'So how did that lead you to her – and us?' Mr Jewels wanted to know. His gem-like eyes held an ugly glitter as he looked over at Caitlin.

'You guys can still hide behind your masks,' Caitlin's voice was bitter as she turned to her fellow vandals. 'And we can be just as sure that he couldn't track me through the Net. He's got to be somebody from my school, who caught on to me in the real world. So you don't have to worry,' she sneered. 'We haven't met out in the flesh since we began this stuff!'

Mr Jewels looked ready to slug the girl, and Matt tensed his muscles, ready for a hopeless defense. But Tex the cartoon cowboy gestured the gleaming Titan back with his oversized six-gun. 'Hold on there, ya big galoot. We're workin' from the other end of the rope right now.'

Once again, Matt noticed the fractional hesitation between moving lips and Western-holo dialog. If that's the Idiom Savant program, it's working even slower than David said it would, he thought. Unless . . . it's not just changing English into that silly lingo, but a completely different language!

But there wasn't time to get into that right now. He had to convince this bunch of spoiled rich kids that he could be useful – and amusing.

'My search kicked out all sorts of rumors about people getting their veeyars trashed, and even roughed up. Now,

I've got a couple of tricks I can pull in virtual – as the lady can tell you.'

'We've heard,' the swordsman said coldly. Matt noticed that he didn't seem to mind that he spoke English with an accent. Unless that accent was some sort of proxy trick . . .

No, Matt told himself. There's not the same sort of hang time on this guy's lips as on the cowboy.

'So you know my kind of stuff can annoy people, even scare them. But it doesn't have the same sort of – authority – you can call on.'

Matt spread out his stick-figure hands. 'With all the rumors I'd collected, I still wasn't sure you guys were for real, or some sort of vapor-tale. So I decided to try and find you. I figured you had to be rich – electronic wilding requires resources.' He rubbed his fingers together in the old gesture for money. 'I also figured you must live pretty close to where you've been playing. That meant getting a line on all the virtual hangouts for rich kids in the D.C. area.'

Matt pinned a smile on his proxy's sketchy face. 'Somehow, I just had a feeling you wouldn't turn out to be a bunch of forty-nine-year-old computer geeks.'

He shrugged. 'And what do you know, I was right. The first site I tried was Maxim's. And who do I meet there but the lovely CeeCee, who talked a little, then slugged the real Courtney Vance when she turned up to complain. I heard the punch, I saw Courtney react in pain . . . and I knew I'd found what I was looking for.'

Matt held up his proxy hand. 'I'm not going to tell you how I connected CeeCee with Caitlin Corrigan. Every relationship needs a little mystery. But I do want you to know that I'm way impressed – and I want in.'

'Look here, pilgrim,' the cartoon cowboy began, spouting his silly Wild West jargon again, 'I don't rightly think you realize who holds the whip hand, here. You tracked us down, right enough. But one shot from my trusty forty-five, and you're pushin' up daisies on Boot Hill. Dead men tell no tales.'

'I'll say it again,' Matt said, hoping his voice was holding steady. 'I don't want to turn you in, I don't want to blackmail you. All I want is to join your team – to learn how you do what you do.'

'Then you'd know more than any of us,' the frog muttered.

Matt was confused, but he couldn't let that show. He *had* to win this bunch over. But how?

The words burst out almost before he realized he was speaking. 'You're worried about me telling tales? If I ran with you, I'd be in for as much trouble as you catch.'

'Maybe.' Mr Jewels drawled the word out as if he were tasting it, thinking over Matt's offer. 'I daresay you've shown that you know your way around computers, since you got this close to us. But that's not all you need to prove if you want to run with us.'

'Meaning what?' Matt asked cautiously.

'You have to be able to pull your weight.' The monolithic jewel-monster leaned forward, his words coming faster. 'Get us in somewhere we haven't been able to penetrate.'

A test, Matt thought. That made a certain sort of sense. At least it would let him get out of this empty white room without getting shot.

'I'm willing to try,' Matt promised. 'As long as it's not

outright impossible, like the Pentagon or the White House.'

'Oh, it's more possible than that.' Mr Jewels gave a grating laugh. 'We want to get into the veeyar of Sean McArdle – he's the son of the Irish ambassador. I'm sure I don't need to tell you more. You can find out all you want to know with a data search.'

'I'll start right away.' Matt hesitated before he went on. 'You all want to get in there?'

The other laughed. 'And walk into a bloody trap? I think not,' Mr Jewels sneered. 'No, all you need to worry about is yourself – and CeeCee here.' He made an ironic bow toward the furious Cat Corrigan.

'Since she's the only one you know out of our little group, you can contact her when you've arranged something.' Mr Jewels turned his gemstone eyes full on Matt. 'If we've heard nothing from you in – oh, a week's time, we'll simply take it for granted that you're no longer interested. But if we hear any rumors about our activities – or detect any official interest in Caitlin, then we'll be forced to interest ourselves in you.'

He loomed over Matt's insubstantial proxy. 'You wouldn't like that, Yank. No, not at all.'

Matt was glad to let Caitlin take him out of there. But when he came to leave her veeyar, he didn't go straight home. Instead, he took a complicated, pre-programmed escape route that shunted him with dizzying speed between dozens of different Net sites. He'd done the same thing when he'd bailed out of Lara Fortune's party, ricocheting back and forth across the Net to baffle any possible tracers that might have been planted on him. He'd even taken the precaution of making this route different from the one he'd taken on Friday night.

His last stop brought him to a huge pyramid ablaze with electrical impulses – the virtual representation of an online catalog operation. The restless glitter represented constant calls for pricing information and orders.

Matt hurtled onward without even slowing, blending into the blaze of electronic activity around the construct. If the video vandals had managed to keep track of him up to now, the sheer volume of information glaring would confuse their pursuit.

He was aiming for a tiny dark spot on the side of the pyramid – a few gigabytes of computer memory which Matt had diverted from the catalog business. Instead, the little niche held programs to let Matt run a self-check to ensure he'd made a clean getaway.

The tiny dark space suddenly flared into life, blinking brightly as the anti-tracking programs gave him a green light, then erased themselves. He took one more whirl around the pyramid, routed himself along with some outgoing calls, and veered off homeward.

Matt's knees felt a little rubbery when he got out of his computer-link chair. Maybe that evasive pattern he'd flown from Vandal Central had a few *too* many twists and turns. His only regret was that he hadn't been able to plant a tracing device in the veeyar where Caitlin had taken him.

That problem was, a bug would turn out to be a two-edged sword. It would reveal the node where the virtual vandals had met, but the transmission would let the bad guys pinpoint him. And right now, the only things he had going were the Caitlin Corrigan connection and his hidden identity.

Matt walked off his shivers, then headed down the hall to the phone.

Now it's my turn to try and unmask a few proxies, he thought as he punched in Captain Winters's office number. Luckily, the captain was in, spending his Saturday clearing away paperwork.

'Captain, it's Matt Hunter,' Matt said into the handset. 'Could I come down there and talk with you? I may have come across a connection to that Camden Yards thing.'

'You don't want to tell me right now? Or e-mail a report?' the officer asked.

Matt coughed. 'I'd rather you hear this in person, sir. When you do, I think you might agree.' No way was he going to talk on an open phone line – or send a message through the virtual vandals' network playground.

A sigh came over the phone. 'I was hoping to leave in a little while – when can you get here?'

'I'm leaving right now,' Matt said.

On the autobus ride to the captain's office in the Pentagon government office center, Matt tried to organize his experiences of the last week into a coherent report. But even his best effort didn't sound so coherent when he faced the impatient Captain Winters.

The captain was a lot less impatient and much more worried by the time Matt finished. 'You're suggesting that the daughter of the Honorable Senator from Massachusetts is linked to a group of wealthy virtual thrill-seekers? And several other members of this bunch are foreign – possibly related to the diplomatic community?'

'I think—' Matt began.

But Captain Winters finished his sentence for him. '*I think you'd better have some pretty convincing evidence to back up charges like that.* We don't have any official standing in the case – it's still the Baltimore PD's baby.' He rolled his eyes. 'And they'd just *love* hearing this theory.'

'I still think the foreign connection thing is worth looking into,' Matt said quietly.

'As long as you don't go rocking any boats,' Winters said. He glanced at his watch. 'I'll leave you to it.' Turning to his computer console, he said, 'Computer, identify for voice commands.'

'Voice identified as Captain James Winters,' the computer responded.

'Open database search, nonclassified material, Corrigan, Caitlin – known associates, specifically foreign nationals.'

'Going back to six months ago?' Matt suggested. 'I don't think they've been meeting recently.'

The captain nodded. 'Time variable extending to six months before present date. Datascrip copy to be presented to Matthew Hunter, identified now.'

'Matthew Hunter,' Matt said.

'Execute,' Captain Winters ordered. He glanced at Matt. 'I'm sure you'll have a bit of a wait. Even for our computer system, this will be a long search.' He went to the door. 'I'll leave this locked. Just close it on the way out. And tell me if anything interesting kicks out.'

Standing alone in the office, Matt impatiently waited as the Net Force search engines ground through all the public information sites – print news, electronic info, HoloNet, and government public affairs – for any connections between Caitlin and Washington's large foreign community.

But impatience quickly became dismay as the computer announced hundreds of hits.

'Organize by individuals,' he ordered, 'listing by name in decreasing frequency of references.'

Even that way, the datascrip Captain Winters had left was quickly filled.

I bet he figured this would happen, Matt thought, and set it up as a lesson for me.

He was about to pull the scrip from its reader when he suddenly stopped, struck by a new thought. He hadn't been able to identify the accents of two of the three proxied-up characters he'd met today. But he had a suspicion about Mr Jewels.

'Separate file,' Matt ordered the computer. 'First ten individuals on the list – sort by nationality. If there are any British subjects, give them precedence.'

The scrip whirred again. 'Last thirty-seven names on master list deleted to make room for file,' the computer warned.

'Accepted,' Matt said. 'List nationality file.'

A holo-screen appeared in the air over the computer console. Matt examined the glowing letters. 'One British subject,' he muttered. 'Look at all those press references.'

Matt decided to try and press his luck. 'Computer,' he said, 'is there a current government file on—' he squinted, then read the guy's name – 'Gerald Savage?'

The room was silent for a moment as the computer searched the Net Force files. 'Affirmative.'

'Is the file classified?'

'Negative.'

'Call up file on Gerald Savage,' Matt ordered.

An eyeblink later, and the image of a harsh-faced but handsome enough guy appeared over the console. There was just a little too much nose and chin, and the brown hair was worn defiantly long.

'Hunh,' Matt muttered. 'It's a State Department, not a Net Force file.'

He frowned as he ordered a scroll of the written contents. Gerald Savage, it seemed, was the kind of guy who gave the idea of diplomatic immunity a bad name. He'd gotten into several physical confrontations, which had earned him the nickname of 'Gerry the Savage.'

Matt became more interested as he discovered that Savage's brawling apparently had a political origin. His father was a radical British politician, campaigning on an angrily anti-Irish platform. Matt knew there had always been a lot of anger in the history of England and Ireland. The Irish had fought for hundreds of years to be free from British rule.

But the antagonistic relationship had taken a new turn since the late 1990s, when Ireland began out-performing Britain economically. Where Englishmen had once claimed superiority, they now felt envy. And Cliff Savage, Gerald's father, had ridden that wave to sudden political prominence.

It looked as though the government had given him a foreign service post to get him out of the country.

Matt shook his head. But why send him here? They had to know about the huge Irish-American community. Or was that the idea? Maybe the people in London were hoping that the Savages would cause some kind of international incident.

'Close file,' Matt ordered. But he was already frowning as a new thought came to him. Caitlin Corrigan. That had to be an Irish name. What was she doing with a guy who liked to dump on Irish people?

Maybe it was just part of Washington society. It was amazing how diplomatic functions were always throwing together people who were supposed to be bitter enemies. Sometimes political points could be made by acting like friends.

Then again, these were two kids whose parents were always in the public eye. Maybe they thought it would be funny to drive their folks crazy by picking the world's most impossible friend.

Matt swallowed. In school, his English class had been going over *Romeo and Juliet*, the famous play where two kids from feuding families had fallen in love.

Any of those scenarios could explain why Caitlin and Gerry the Savage had gotten together. But all they told Matt was that he had a lot more to find out about Cat Corrigan before he'd know what made her tick.

Chapter 7

Matt knew he should be working on the 'assignment' he'd been given by the virtual vandals – that little job he hadn't mentioned to Captain Winters. His attempt at undercover work would go up in smoke if he couldn't deliver on what he'd been asked to do.

Instead, Matt found himself staring at a holo-image over his computer console. It showed Caitlin Corrigan in an evening gown, arriving at some charity event with her escort, Gerald Savage. Cat was giving the paparazzi a mischievous grin. The Savage looked as if he'd just bitten into a chocolate-covered pickle.

How was Matt supposed to compete with these people? They were the innermost in-crowd, invited to every social event. If they couldn't get to Sean McArdle, how could Matt expect to get through?

Unless . . . Matt suddenly thought, maybe I'm asking the wrong question. *Why* can't they get through to Sean McArdle?

He erased the image from his computer console, and began a new data search. As Matt read the news reports he called up, a line of type caught his eyes. Then a slow smile appeared on his face. Maybe, just maybe, there *was* a way . . .

A day or so later, Matt ventured out into the Net, carrying his telecommunications icon, Leif Anderson's proxy program, and Caitlin's earring protocol.

He took a roundabout route before heading to Cat's veeyar, just in case she was monitoring where he came from.

Getting paranoid, aren't we? A little voice asked in the back of his mind.

Maybe he was. But keeping himself anonymous was one of the few advantages he had against these rich kids. He figured keeping that advantage was worth a little work.

Matt flew through the glowing world of the Net until he came to another heavily trafficked data node. Then he transformed himself into Mr Sticks and activated Cat's communications protocol. Again he flew through the walls of the Corrigans' virtual mansion and into the endless surreal landscape of Caitlin's personal veeyar.

Cat appeared a moment later, wearing jeans and a sweater. Her feet were bare, and Matt noticed that her eyes seemed puffy.

'Are you okay?' he asked.

'Oh, I'm just great,' she retorted. 'My whole life is in the hands of a guy who dresses like a squiggle, so I have to jump like a trained seal whenever he shows up.'

She rubbed her hands over her face, sighing. 'I'm sorry. I was out last night – late. It felt as if I'd just closed my eyes for a nap when my beeper announced that you were in here.'

Matt actually found himself feeling sorry for Caitlin. *Wait a minute*, he told himself. She wasn't forced to get into this. Remember Leif – and the other people who got hurt because she felt she needed a little excitement in her life.

He pushed his sympathy away. 'I think I've got a way to get at Sean McArdle, just as your friends wanted. It will be tomorrow, if you need to get anything ready. And you'll need this.'

Matt tossed Caitlin a small program icon.

When she caught it, her virtual image began to transform. Cat's shining blond hair turned mousy-brown, shrinking back into a severe haircut, which even though it was short, made her hair look stringy. Her heart-shaped face lengthened, the cheeks sinking in, her jaw growing long. Her lips flattened out into a tight line, and her eyes went from blue to a washed-out hazel.

The sweater and jeans morphed into a baggy, unflattering jumper dress covering a cheap, plain white blouse. Bony wrists and nail-bitten hands stuck out from the too-short cuffs. Matchstick legs and ugly brown shoes emerged from the too-long skirt.

Caitlin looked down at her altered self and let off a horrified scream.

'My hair! My clothes . . . the rest of me! What did you do?' she demanded.

'Don't burst a valve,' Matt told her. 'It's just a proxy. You'll need it to get in – just as I'll need this.'

He activated his proxy program, turning into a gangly red-headed boy with a freckled baby-face, wearing a not-quite-clean white shirt, a too-short tie, and dress pants that were a good inch and a half too short, showing off white gym socks.

Caitlin looked at him and shuddered. 'Tell me that's not the way you actually look,' she begged. 'You'd make a perfect Dexter.'

She called up a virtual mirror and stood beside him, examining their reflections. 'And you turned me into a real Nerdetta.'

'So nobody would expect that's you under there – or me.' Matt tapped the rumpled tie on his proxy-self's chest. 'But they'd think we look exactly like a pair of serious junior reporters from our school newspaper.'

Cat's altered face turned to him, her eyes sharp. 'Newspaper?'

'I bet you and your friends tried the usual social angles that work with diplomatic brats,' Matt said. 'But Sean McArdle doesn't go out to play – or bring people in for virtual bashes like Lara Fortune's. No, he's kind of serious, a real – what did you call it? – a Dexter. He uses the Net for research, not for playing. But he does open up his system for one thing that I bet your pals never thought about. Once a month, he hosts a virtual youth press conference. That's what's happening tomorrow. It took a little foozling on the school computers, but I got us clearance to attend as reporters for the *Bradford Bulletin*.'

'I usually erase that thing right after it's downloaded to our computers,' Caitlin admitted.

Unless it's got an article about a big dance, or some nonsense about one of your Leet friends, Matt thought.

Out loud, he just cleared his throat. 'I'll be Ed Noonan, and you'll be Cathy Carty. Here's some ID and your clearance.' He handed over a couple of other icons.

'Cathy – sounds like Cat. Good thinking,' Caitlin said. 'Is

the name you've chosen close to your real one?'

Matt just gave her a sour smile. 'These people don't exist, so there'll be nothing to connect us to them – or to the real newspaper. I've chosen Irish names, because I figured that's the kind of journalist who'd want to go to an Irish kid's press conference.'

'What's he going to talk about?' Cat wondered.

'I have no idea,' Matt admitted. 'We'll just have to go, wave a pair of recorders around, and try to keep a straight face, no matter what.'

'It *will* be different,' Caitlin admitted.

'The conference will be held tomorrow afternoon after school,' Matt said. 'What do you want to do, meet here?'

Caitlin deactivated the proxy program, transforming back to her natural self. 'Might as well,' she said, coiling her long blond hair around one finger. 'But we won't go directly to the veeyar from here.'

She gave Matt another one of her bitter smiles. 'I've got a list of good cutout locations. Tonight, I'll choose one and set it up. It should cover us in case someone takes it into his or her head to backtrace people coming in.'

'Good thinking,' Matt said, his voice flat. 'I'll see you tomorrow, then.'

When he arrived at Cat's veeyar the next day, she was already wearing the plain-Jane virtual form Matt had engineered for her.

'Oh, it's me all right,' she assured Matt, her bony face squinching up in disgust as she looked down at herself. 'Trust me, none of the guys would want to wear this.'

Caitlin picked up a virtual tote-bag – an awful-looking

thing that fit right in with her unfashionable appearance. 'Ready to go?'

Matt had already adopted the Ed Noonan proxy before arriving. 'Why not?' he said.

Caitlin held out her hand, and Matt took it. They flashed across the Net, coming to rest in a large, very realistic simulated room with a series of stone-topped tables facing a raised platform with a lecture desk, also stone-topped.

Matt released the girl's hand. 'Wait a minute!' he said. 'This is the virtual chemistry lab at Bradford!'

Caitlin chuckled. 'You aren't the only one who can foozle the school's computers.'

Matt gave a wordless grunt. The guy had managed to route a request through the school's system. Whoever was behind the virtual vandals had completely invaded the computers in Bradford Academy!

'Come on!' Cat checked the dowdy, old-fashioned watch her proxy was wearing. 'We're going to be late if you keep fooling around.'

Sighing, Matt took Caitlin's hand again as she routed them to the press conference using the clearance protocols he had obtained.

Matt had wondered if the Irish Embassy's Net node would turn out to have shamrocks, or be designed in the shape of a quaint cottage. It was almost a disappointment to find that the official site was a typical ultramodern virtual office setup.

They were quickly routed to Sean McArdle's veeyar, which was configured as a large lecture hall. Matt was impressed at the number of young journalists who had gathered. 'We're going to wind up at the back,' he whispered to Caitlin.

'All the better,' she muttered.

Matt blinked. Then again, Cat was probably right. They could just hang out and listen, away from all the action.

Even so, he was surprised that Cat didn't take a seat, just standing in the rear.

Exactly on the dot of the hour, Sean McArdle appeared at the podium. He was a tall, intense, shy young man who was obviously terrified at the idea of getting up to speak in front of a crowd. But for some reason – maybe to get over that terror – here he was, conducting a general interview.

McArdle's voice cracked as he introduced himself, and he gave a sudden, disarming grin. 'Don't think I'll ever get this speech-making thing right,' he said. 'A terrible failing if I ever hope to become a politician.'

But as he went on to talk about Ireland and its economic achievements, Matt had to admit that if McArdle wasn't a politician, he made a great cheerleader. The young man was definitely proud of his country and where it had gone. 'When my father was growing up, we were still accepting handouts from the members of the European Economic Community,' he said. 'The joke in those days was "Thank heavens for the German taxpayers," because they were paying for the roads and infrastructure to bring us up to speed. I know quite a few of you are descended from Irish immigrants. So I think you'll know what I mean when I say that certain people – certain *countries* – always pushed the idea that our people were shiftless – lazy. But thirty years ago, we 'lazy Irish' had some of the best-educated young people in Europe. We were getting some of the plum jobs in that country which will remain nameless, becoming involved in computer design, even working on parts of the American space program.'

McArdle gestured around the virtual meeting hall they now occupied. 'We've been very involved in the Net. All the constructs at this node – including this veeyar – were programmed by Irish engineers. If you like this meeting setup, I'm allowed to give you a copy.'

Now that he was up and talking, a flush of color appeared on his high, prominent cheekbones.

'An affluent economy led to some problems we'd never have anticipated – like a flood of illegal immigrants. We aren't a large country, and for centuries we've been a single people. That's made it difficult for would-be refugees to fit in – and everyone hasn't had the training to share in our prosperity. I know that's led to some bitterness from people fleeing the strife in the Balkans. But especially in recent years, Ireland has taken the lead in bringing development money to that region, helping to build up the business climate as our economic partners did for us.'

As he began to bring on the holo-clips, images, charts and graphs, young Sean McArdle now seemed completely comfortable with his speech-making.

Maybe he will make it as a politician back home, Matt thought. *But now I'm getting bored.*

He glanced round at Caitlin to see how she was taking the presentation. With her political family, she probably heard stuff like this all the time.

She stood with her back to the rear wall, half-hidden in the shadows, not even bothering to listen.

In fact, she seemed to be fiddling with something in her

hands. Matt looked a little closer. What was that? A sticky label?

That seemed to be exactly what she was fooling with. Even as he took a step toward her, she peeled the backing from the label and slapped it onto the wall behind her.

Matt strained his eyes, trying to read whatever it was she'd stuck up.

It seemed pretty silly to him, pushing so hard to get in somewhere if all she wanted to do was a bit of petty vandalism. It would probably turn out to be some nasty anti-Irish slogan spouted by Gerald Savage. What would it do? Glare out in intolerable brightness? Or maybe give off smoke?

Instead, the slapped-on label did something even weirder. Its color shifted, chameleon-like, until it matched the dark green of the wall itself. Rather than standing out, the sticker seemed to be hiding itself.

Matt came closer, trying to find the blasted thing.

But the label was vanishing . . . not blending in against the virtual paint job, but *melting in to become part of the wall itself!*

Chapter 8

'What *is* it?' Caitlin hissed as Matt dashed up – and roughly pushed her aside. 'What are you doing?' she demanded, sounding more scared than angry.

He paid no attention, scratched simulated nail-bitten fingers along the wall. Nothing! The sticky label he had seen Cat slap onto the green paint had left no trace.

Correction, Matt thought. It left no *visible* trace. The blasted thing had somehow become one with this simulated room. Oh, it was possible that the Irish designers' programming had simply erased an element that didn't belong. But these are virtual vandals we're dealing with, Matt thought. Whoever they've got behind them, I can't believe the Genius' handiwork could disappear so easily. Unless it was *built* to do that.

He turned cold eyes on Caitlin Corrigan. 'That label you were fiddling with – that's a program icon, isn't it? Removing the backing – that started the program. Now it's eased its way into the coding for this simulation – probably for the whole veeyar.'

He caught the flash of terror in her eyes. Even as he wondered *why* she was getting so upset over what he'd realized, his hand darted out to grab her by the arm.

That was a lucky move. Just as he established contact with her, Cat bailed out of the press conference.

Because he was holding on, Matt followed along as they rocketed wildly through the Net.

Caitlin tried to peel him off, dragging him through roaring rivers of daytime data exchange. Even with flextime, the hours of nine to five were still the heaviest times for information passage.

Matt hung on for dear life as they bounced around like a pinball moving at light-speed. Now he had two questions he really wanted an answer for. What was in that weird label-program she'd left in Sean McArdle's veeyar? And why would simply asking about it result in this frenzied attempt to run away?

Cat was gulping in air as if she'd been running for miles – or was she simply sobbing? Finally, they pinwheeled in to a familiar setting.

They were back in the virtual chem lab at Bradford Academy.

'You know,' Matt said, 'my lab partner managed to make a mistake in here that would have blown us up out in reality. Instead, we got caught in a system freeze and had all our chemicals deleted from the simulation.' He paused. 'And, of course, everybody in the class laughed at us because of the big red warning label that appeared – "UNSTABLE REACTION INITIATED." They called us the Unstable Boys for weeks, until somebody else got shut down for spilling hydrochloric acid down the front of his shirt. I guess we were lucky. People still call this guy by the nickname "Bernie" – for the acid burns.'

Caitlin crouched against one of the stone-topped laboratory tables, her eyes closed. 'Just get your hands off. Let me go, will you?' she begged.

'I told you those stories to show that anybody can make a mistake,' Matt said gently. 'Didn't you think I'd ask about that stick-on program if I saw you use it? It's pretty ingenious, after all. Subtle. Not exactly the style of your jeweled-up pal or that cartoon cowboy, I'd think. Was it whipped up by that guy who morphed me from a giant frog into a fancy swordsman?'

Still resting her cheek against the cool stone tabletop Caitlin stared at him wide-eyed. 'I can't tell you! I *can't*!'

'You mean you have to talk it out with your friends, first?' Matt said. 'I can live with that.'

'Just let me be!' Tears sparkled in Caitlin's eyes and began streaking across her cheek.

Matt couldn't stand watching the girl cry. He relaxed his grip on her arm.

Instantly, she disappeared.

Nice going, he told himself sourly. *That's two experiments you've blown in here. It's lucky the monitoring program isn't on, or there'd be big red letters glaring around me now.* He could just imagine the error message: SOFT-HEARTED JERK.

Matt quickly bailed out of the virtual chemistry lab – it was forbidden territory except for working classes. He'd have been in a lot of trouble if he'd gotten caught in there. Still playing it safe, he visited another busy Net node before returning to his home veeyar.

The more he thought about it, the more he became

convinced that there was someone behind the virtual vandals he'd seen. Whoever it might be, this Genius just about scared the fertilizer out of Caitlin Corrigan. In comparison, she'd been downright calm when her friends had threatened to silence Matt permanently. She'd even been cool when Mr Jewels – Gerry the Savage – had loomed over her, threatening Cat with a pounding.

What was it about whoever created their programs? Why did that person fill Caitlin with such terror that she just wanted to run away?

Matt couldn't be absolutely sure about his suspicions. He'd have to dig deeper into Gerald Savage's background, find out how much programming the English kid knew. Somehow, he'd also have to unmask the other characters and do the same with them. It had been a gut feeling, saying that the stick-label program seemed too subtle next to the proxies the three boys were using.

But then, maybe somebody really subtle would be able to hide behind an obvious mask . . .

Matt reached his home veeyar, broke the connection, and sat slumped in his computer-link chair. He could play what-if and maybe until he grew a long gray beard. What Net Force needed was to get a little hands-on with some of the other side's programming.

He got out of the chair and went to the phone, just managing to catch Captain Winters. The captain was *not* delighted to hear from him.

'Are you now suggesting that the son of the Irish ambassador is involved with this bunch?' he demanded.

'No, sir. I think he may be a *target*. He has a very open veeyar. It's used for junior press conferences—'

'And it's protected by diplomatic immunity,' Winters cut in.

'I think the programming may have been corrupted,' Matt went on. 'Maybe you could try an unofficial approach, tell them you've heard about the press conferences, and express interest in the programming behind them. They give out copies of the program. If you ask for recordings of recent conferences, you might get a reproduction of the corrupted coding.'

Captain Winters gave a short, irritated grunt. 'It might be worth a try,' he admitted. 'Let me make the contact, and we'll see what happens.'

The phone rang just as the Hunter family was sitting down for dinner. Matt's mother answered from the kitchen extension, putting down the platter of protein burgers she'd prepared. 'Hello? Oh, yes, Captain. He's right here.'

She passed the phone to Matt, then pointed to the tray.

Matt got the message. 'Hello, Captain Winters. We're just sitting down to supper—'

'Then I'll keep it brief,' the captain said brusquely. 'Looks like you were right about that program corruption. I got a copy from the Irish embassy and sent it down to Quantico. Our technicians there found an entire section of coding that doesn't belong. It looks like an old-fashioned trapdoor program, allowing access to the simulation and the computer hardware from outside.'

'Really?' Matt said in surprise. 'But I thought modern programming made that sort of setup impossible?'

'Not anymore,' the captain said grimly. 'It may be an old-fashioned idea, but whoever whomped this up has managed to evade even the newest security routines.' He paused for a second. 'There are lots of people at Net Force who'd very much like to talk with this person.'

'If I find anything out, Captain, I'll be sure to let you know.'

Captain Winters made a noise that sounded suspiciously like a 'Humph!' Then he said, 'I guess that's all we can ask for. Good night, Matt.'

'Good night, sir.' Matt hung up the phone and picked at dinner until his father bundled up the dishes and began washing them. Matt dried, then went to his room – and his computer-link chair.

Again, Matt waited until he'd reached a busy Net node before he donned Leif Anderson's Mr Sticks proxy. Then he activated Cat Corrigan's communications protocol and streaked across the neon wonderland. Yes, he was coming up on the government Net areas. Then he veered off into quieter neighborhood of the rich and well-connected.

There was a glowing version of Mount Vernon, dead ahead.

He rocketed straight for the glowing wall . . . and crashed.

Matt huddled on the cushions of his computer-link chair, holding onto his head as if he feared it was about to fall off. His teeth were gritted together so tightly, the muscles in his jaw ached. But he didn't want to yell, didn't want to bring his parents in.

Pain seemed to be pounding along every neuron in his brain. He'd experienced system crashes before, and this was no worse than any of them. Certainly, he was better off than

Leif Anderson had been after being hit by that virtual bullet.

Matt was conscious, and breathing . . . and aware of every twinge racing around his nervous system. He knew that the fizzling pain would die away. By the time he woke up tomorrow morning, all he'd have was a mild headache.

What really hurt was the way he'd been cut off from Caitlin Corrigan.

Man, Matt thought. *When she doesn't want to answer questions, she certainly lets you know!*

Chapter 9

Even a night's sleep hadn't completely erased the headache from Matt's crash – literal and figurative – with Cat Corrigan's system. As he rode to school on the autobus, Matt daydreamed about confronting the girl, grabbing her, giving her a good shaking. Didn't she know he was trying to help her?

Annoyed, Matt shook his head – and wished he hadn't. *Of course* she didn't know he was trying to help her. He really wasn't. He was trying to track down the virtual vandals who'd caused such chaos and hurt Leif Anderson. Was he getting turned around because one of those vandals turned out to be pretty . . . and scared?

Besides, there was no way he could confront Caitlin without giving away his identity. Not unless he wanted to give a new target to this bunch of nuts who could shoot people in holoform.

But, with Caitlin hiding out from him, he'd lost any chance of unmasking the other members of the group.

Or had he?

Prep period seemed louder than usual, thanks to Matt's continuing headache. But he pushed that aside, waving over

Andy Moore and David Gray.

'Idiots,' Andy growled. His sunburnt face had reached the peeling stage, and he was pretty annoyed that some classmates had hung the nickname 'Scab' on him. Between anger and the remaining burn, his face looked redder than ever.

'Keep that up, and they'll start calling you "Tomato," ' David warned. 'Besides, you've stuck some people with a few nicknames. If you dish it out—'

'Yeah, I know, I'm supposed to take it,' Andy grumbled. 'But that doesn't say anything about having to *like* it.'

He grinned at Matt. 'So how's the big investigation going? I figured that's why you dragged us over – especially since we barely heard a word from you after Saturday. Have you been spending all your time with . . . Caitlin?'

Andy made the girl's name sound incredibly gooey, finishing with a romantic sigh.

Matt didn't know whether to be embarrassed or angry. 'Get over it!' he snapped. 'I'm trying to get a line on the three guys who are in the group.'

'You mean Caitlin hasn't told you yet?' Andy asked pointedly.

'Why not give it a rest, Scab?' David said. Then, ignoring Andy, he turned to Matt. 'What can I do to help?'

'Hey, don't be like that,' Andy said quickly. 'I want to help, too.'

Matt pulled two datascrips from his school bag. Each contained copies of the file Matt had gotten from the Net Force computers – the diplomatic brats who'd been in contact with Cat Corrigan.

'I've got two lists on these – one tallies a couple of

hundred foreign guys who've been seen with Caitlin Corrigan. The other is the top ten listing of diplo-brats who know her. What I need to know is how many of these guys would qualify as hackers.'

Matt scowled. '*Somebody* had to come up with the programming that lets the virtual vandals do what they do. They didn't buy it in their friendly neighborhood MicroShop.'

Andy's eyebrows zoomed toward his hairline. 'So you think the kick-butt program was developed by a mad genius on Diplomatic Row?'

'I don't know,' Matt admitted. 'But I do know that the other vandals seem to be foreigners. One's a Brit, another speaks with some kind of European accent. And the third doesn't seem to speak English at all. So I've got two sorting jobs to do—'

'I call dibs on checking the language thing!' Andy swiftly said. 'I'm betting there aren't many people in diplomatic circles nowadays who can't speak English. It's the lingo everybody uses in international politics and business. Who'd want to have an ambassador standing around like a dummy?'

'So you figure that sort of diplomat would . . . stand out?' David asked.

Andy nodded smugly.

'Of course, with that kind of handicap, an ambassador might want to keep his ignorance a secret,' David went on.

Andy suddenly looked nervous.

'On the other hand, computer courses or awards should be a matter of public record.' David gave his pal a big, cheerful grin. 'Gee, I'm so glad *I* got offered the easy job.'

Matt was still chuckling as he headed for his first-period class.

There wasn't much else for Matt to enjoy during the day. With all the investigation he'd been doing, his classwork had suffered. It seemed word immediately went out on Teacher-Net, because every class instructor seemed to find some way to drag him over the coals.

At lunch, Sandy Braxton was sympathetic. 'Mr Fairlie really nailed you today,' the rich kid said. 'I thought he only saved those kinds of zinger for me.' Sandy started to laugh, but cut off in mid-chuckle. 'I hope our project isn't distracting you too much.'

More likely, he's now worrying that I'm going to mess up whatever part *he* doesn't, Matt thought.

Whatever his worry, Sandy seemed to forget it as he talked about something he'd discovered in his research on the Battle of Gettysburg. It turned out he had an ancestor who'd fought at the battle. 'My great-great-great-great-great-grandfather joined a Virginia regiment and fought until Gettysburg,' Sandy said. 'He got his arm shot off.'

'Did it happen during Pickett's Charge?' Matt asked. If he remembered correctly, the general had led Virginian troops on his ill-fated attack.

'Nah. Great-whatever-grandpa was hit during the first day of the battle.'

'Oh,' Matt said. It was easy to see how Sandy got distracted into the gossipy side of history. Maybe he was interested in society gossip, too?

Matt decided to see. 'Hey, Sandy, I've been hearing rumors about something weird going on among the diplomatic brats in town. Do you know anything about it?'

The other boy only shrugged, shaking his head. 'My family doesn't have much to do with the diplomatic corps,' he said. 'Except my daddy made a bunch of money off some of them. He's developing a gated community down by the Anacostia River. Thought there'd be a bunch of folks from Capitol Hill who'd move in. Instead, it's like wall-to-wall ambassadors. Not that Daddy minds.' Sandy gave him a big, slow smile. 'Money is money, no matter what country it comes from.'

At home after school, Matt tried to do some of the research for his joint paper with Sandy. But he kept slipping back to the list of ambassadors' kids, as if just a little more study might unlock some hidden secret.

One thing he noticed was that the addresses seemed to clump together into two bunches, one in a zip code for northwest Washington, the other for a zip code in the southwest.

Matt knew that most of the embassies clustered in D.C.'s northwest corner. Could all these southwest addresses represent foreign families who'd moved to the development Sandy had talked about?

Setting a search engine to work on the question, Matt was a little shocked at the number of hits that quickly showed up. He asked for an overview, and an article titled 'Population Shift – Washington, D.C.' appeared in holoform over his computer console. Browsing through, Matt learned how the Federal government and private developers had changed the face of the city over the years. One of the things that surprised him most was an old flatfilm picture taken less than a hundred years ago. It showed the dome of the Capitol building rising over the backyard laundry of a beat-up wooden house that looked like something out of a hillbilly comedy.

Matt couldn't believe that such an eyesore would have been tolerated on Capitol Hill. Now it was the site of an old office building and underground parking garage. Still, the area southwest of the Capitol had been the home to very poor people for fifty years after that picture had been taken. Pockets of poverty had remained even after the turn of the century.

The article even showed pictures of the new gated community, a place called Gardens of Carrolsbury after an old town located on the site before the city of Washington had even been laid out. Matt had to laugh when he discovered that in its poorer days, the place had been called Buzzard Point.

He closed out the article and went back to staring at the list of names when his computer began beeping – a file transfer was underway.

It was David, reporting in. His search for computer wizards among the diplomatic community had clicked with very few people on the list connected with Cat Corrigan. High on David's computer-geek list was Sean McArdle, the Irish ambassador's son. Matt noticed that he lived in the Gardens of Carrolsbury.

But it seemed that Caitlin didn't get along with real hacker types.

Probably thinks of them being as Dexters, Matt thought, running down the list. There were just a couple of names, none of them in the top ten.

David included a file on how Gerald Savage boasted

about being almost computer-illiterate. Apparently, that was a swipe at all the Irish programmers invading the British job market. David had thought it was pretty funny, but Matt wasn't laughing. That sort of ignorance – and taking pride in it – was entirely in character for Gerry the Savage.

Matt frowned as he continued to study the two lists, plus the clipping and head shot of Gerald Savage.

'Computer,' he suddenly said. 'Prepare search engine Newshound. Search nonclassified media databases for any references to associates of Gerald Savage. Emphasis on violence and pranks. Sort by frequency of reference. Then compare with present lists.'

Sighing, Matt further ordered the computer to work in the background while projecting the datascrip Sandy Braxton had given him. Might as well get some reading done, Matt told himself. All that searching and sorting will take a long time.

Matt had moved on to doing homework when the computer beeped again. The job wasn't done – instead, it was Andy Moore sending an electronic file. Not surprisingly, Andy's report was a lot more casual than David's.

Yo, Matt!

D.G. was right. Ambassadors do not like to admit they don't know English.

But there were two exceptions in the diplo-brat department – kids who might reasonably expect to be using Idiom Savant.

Back when smash-dancing was hot, Cat went out with a German guy named Gunter Mohler. Good choice for a partner if you're doing something that's half-dance, half-karate. He's built like a mix between a football linebacker and an autotruck.

Seems he was brought up by his widowed mom to be a 'true German' – so he only speaks the tongue of his forefathers. That must be an annoyance for his stepfather, who's a trade attaché at the embassy.

Then there's Serge Woronov, whose father is the ambassador from Slobodan Narodny, the new Balkan Free State. You know how fiercely nationalistic they are in that part of the world. Foreign languages are strictly zabranjeno – *forbidden – especially for anyone with political ambitions.*

These are the only two I've been able to find out about. Hope it helps.

Matt was chuckling, shaking his head, when the computer beeped yet again.

A quick glance at the holo-display showed that his search had been completed.

'Okay,' Matt muttered. 'Let's check out *all* these lists.'

It was like those Venn diagrams in school. While each suspect might have a wide circle of friends, Matt was only checking where those circles overlapped. There were still a lot of people, but there were a lot fewer.

Matt scowled. Andy's list wasn't too helpful, after all. Both Gunter Mohler and Serge Woronov appeared on both the Savage and Corrigan pal rosters.

Another name on both lists caught Matt's attention. It seemed strangely familiar. 'Computer,' he ordered. 'Subject Lucien Valery. Recent media references.'

The computer holo flickered, then showed a story about a prank involving a local fencing instructor. The teacher had penalized a French fencer – Lucien Valery – while refereeing a competition. When he went to drive home, the official had been caught by a dye bomb which marked his skin red, white, and blue – the color of the French flag.

Valery had been suspected of setting the joke bomb, since he had a long history of pulling pranks. But nothing had been proven – perhaps because he was the son of a French diplomat. Anyway, the prank backfired – Lucien Valery lost a chance to try out for his country's Olympic fencing team.

A Frenchman, Matt thought. If people wanted to use an insulting nickname, they'd call him a 'Frog.'

Immediately, he thought of the six-foot frog who'd confronted him when he'd met the virtual vandals.

It couldn't be – could it?

But then, Lucien Valery had shown himself to possess a weird sense of humor. When the frog had wanted to threaten him, it had changed into an old-time swordsman . . . and Lucien Valery knew how to use a sword.

Matt tried to remember what the swordsman had said. Had he spoken with a French accent? The fact was, Matt couldn't remember. He'd been too distracted by the blade at his throat and the cartoon six-gun aimed at his head.

At least now he had a few new suspects to go after.

He also had a new idea. Jumping up, Matt headed for the phone. Maybe he could catch Captain Winters before he left his office for the day.

'Winters,' the captain's voice came over the phone after Matt punched in the number.

'Sir, it's Matt Hunter again. I was wondering about that trapdoor program you found. I'm sure you've had people taking it apart to see exactly how it ticked. Was there anything about it that might seem – well, foreign?'

'Still working on the theory these pranksters are diplomatic dependants, eh, Hunter!' Captain Winters sounded in a much better mood than the last time they'd talked. 'Well, you may be a little disappointed at what the techs told me. The trapdoor we found in the press-conference program was developed on a cheap, bargain-store computer, by someone using obsolete programming tools. Doesn't exactly sound like a rich and privileged diplo-brat, does it?'

'Um – I guess not,' Matt admitted.

'No.' The captain's voice sounded a bit less smug as he went on. 'That programming was as American – and as cheap – as mock apple pie.'

Chapter 10

After saying goodbye to Captain Winters, Matt headed back to his computer. He felt as if the ground had just been cut from under his feet. Even if the captain hadn't gone for his theory about the virtual vandals being bored rich kids, Matt had known he was right.

After all, he'd tracked down Cat Corrigan and proven she was involved. He was pretty sure that Gerald Savage was another of the proxied-up troublemakers. And he had a few suspects from the huge number of diplomatic kids who lived in D.C.

So why would a bunch of kids who pretty much have the world by the tail work their crimes with a bunch of el cheapo programming?

It didn't make sense.

Shutting his eyes, Matt called up memories of the weird wonderland that Caitlin Corrigan used for a veeyar. Everything about it screamed money. He didn't know about the white room where he and Caitlin had gone to see the rest of the group. But the proxies they had used to mask their identities had definitely been expensive – professionally designed, top-dollar simulations. The nerdy school reporters that Matt had come up with were simple and crude compared to what these guys used. But then, his creations didn't have to morph into super-cool swordsmen.

It just didn't make sense.

Could the dirt-cheap programming be another sort of disguise? An attempt to throw off any investigators from looking among the rich, bored kids? It looked as if that had worked with Captain Winters. He was looking for someone American working on an antique computer system.

In that case, whoever was coming up with the software for the virtual vandals had to be an incredible genius. He or she had to be able to step away from cutting-edge machinery and create programs that could boggle the latest technology – while using equipment and tools that most people would consider junk.

And there was still a problem with his hypothetical genius pretending poverty. The members of the group were still their mega-buck proxies when they went out to trash veeyars. No way were the sims they'd worn at Camden Yards quick and dirty disguises.

Matt sighed. There went another good theory down the toilet.

Could there be a practical reason for using what anybody in this country would consider antique equipment? Some Europeans were very thrifty when it came to machinery. In his *Introduction to Computers* class, Matt remembered reading how certain operating systems were still used in European computers years after they'd become extinct in the U.S.A. Maybe Gunter Mohler learned his computing on an ancient system. Or Serge Woronov. Matt knew that there was a tremendous amount of ancient equipment in the

Balkans. Plenty of military computers had been left behind by the various peacekeeping forces serving there over the decades.

However, that would have to mean that Gunter or Serge were crypto-geeks. Could David Gray have missed them in his data search?

There was only one way to find out. Matt got on his computer, sending a message to David:

Have two possible non-English-speaking types. Need to know just how much they know about computers.

He attached the file that Andy had sent and waited to see what David would say.

Shortly afterwards, his computer beeped. David's message was short.

The folks at Slobodan Narodny are a bit paranoid in their computer security. As for the German computers, well, don't ask any questions about how the following file got into your hands.

Matt blinked in surprise as he began reading through the attached file. It seemed to be a form of some kind. The word *Name* had 'Gunter Mohler' filled in beside it. Then came *Address*, and two entries – one of them with a southwest D.C. zip code.

As he read on, less and less of the file made sense. It was in a foreign language – German? – and would have to be translated.

'Computer – auto-translate,' Matt ordered. As the words

began to make sense, he gave a low whistle. Somehow, David had gotten into the German embassy's computer system and retrieved the personal file on Gunter Mohler!

The file was nothing if not thorough. It listed his school grades since kindergarten. Matt sighed when he saw a barely-passing mark in Computer Basics – the bonehead programming course. Mohler began to look less and less like the shadowy genius Matt was trying to track down.

Of course, a computer genius would have no problem changing computer records, Matt told himself. But why would Gunter suspect that anyone might be checking this file?

Matt scanned on through the file, moving ahead of the translation. He had to smile at some of the odd-looking German words. There was one – Krankenhaus. What the heck did that mean?

He watched while the translation program chewed through this section, turning the German words into English. It turned out to deal with Gunter's health. 'Krankenhaus' meant hospital. Gunter had been rushed to an emergency room to have his appendix removed.

Matt's eyes narrowed as he noticed the date. Gunter had been undergoing surgery at just about the same time as the virtual vandals had turned Camden Yards Stadium into chaos.

'So,' Matt muttered, 'it looks like Gunter can't be the Genius . . . *or* one of the vandals.'

Frowning, he sat back in his computer-link chair, closed his eyes, let his implants take over. An instant later, he sat drifting in the air before the floating slab that was his virtual workplace. Good thing he'd finished his classwork. He had a lot of brain-strain ahead if he wanted to turn the vague ideas in his head into real plans.

Matt worked through the evening with only a quick break for dinner and the dishes. It was almost ten o'clock before he decided he was ready. His stomach was tight as he floated in his veeyar, looking at the little line of program icons on the marble slab. On one side was the fiery pawn of Leif's proxy program and the lightning bolt that would take him into the Net. Then there were the programs he'd been working on. A copy of Cat Corrigan's earring lay on the workspace, twisted and tarnished where Matt had been tampering with it. There was also a small white key which Matt had spent a long time programming, and an icon that looked like a tiny set of binoculars.

Last was a small book – an information file filled with everything Matt had discovered or guessed about the virtual vandals. He not only put this into his computer's memory, but also loaded it onto a datascrip. Maybe it was asking for bad luck to act as if he'd never come back from this venture. But he knew his half-baked plan was dangerous, and he wanted the record to remain if the virtual vandals decided to silence him.

Matt took another moment to write up a short virtual message which he'd carry along. He'd been thinking about it all night.

Cat,

Okay, I won't ask where you got the magic label I saw you use. But don't you think I should get a chance to see your friends again?

After all, I did everything you guys asked. I think you ought to keep your promises.

I'll be back at midnight to talk to you. If I find out I can't trust you, don't expect me to keep quiet about it.

Mr Sticks

He turned the message into a little scroll-icon and left it in line with the others. Then, taking a deep breath, he scooped them all up and moved out into the Net.

The virtual constructs seemed much clearer and brighter than they'd ever seemed before – or was that just the condemned man noticing things he'd never paid much attention to before?

Matt darted back and forth across the glowing landscape, whizzing around through several major nodes to keep anyone from backtracking him.

Okay, he thought, no more putting it off. He held up Caitlin's communications protocol – with his modifications – and activated it.

His course to Caitlin's virtual mansion was becoming almost familiar now. Here's where he'd skim the edge of the government's virtual domain . . .

Matt came to a dead stop. This was one of the changes he'd put into Caitlin's program. It had been a nasty enough shock when he'd found himself locked out of her system. Cat had done that on the spur of the moment, scared by his questions. With time to think . . . well, she might have come up with some nastier surprises. Especially with her friends to help.

Sorting through his icons, Matt chose the tiny binoculars.

From here on in, he was going to scout out his route. He didn't think it was likely that Caitlin had gone to the government, but better safe than sorry.

His program scanned the constructs ahead, trying to find anything that looked like a disguised security coding.

Matt smiled. Nothing.

He slowly continued on the route that Caitlin had given him, still checking for computerized watchdogs or virtual guards. At last he reached the edge of the grounds that surrounded the glowing copy of Mount Vernon.

Everything still looked clean.

Matt dashed for the wall which held the secret trapdoor to Caitlin's veeyar. But instead of crashing into it again, he braked sharply. Then, holding Cat's earring and his message in his right hand, he began slowly pushing it into the wall.

His tinkering with the communications protocol worked! Instead of crashing the program, the virtual wall in front of him seemed to give way. His tampering wasn't perfect. Matt felt as if he were shoving his hand through clay or soggy sand. But he was able to get through and leave his message in Caitlin's veeyar.

At first, Matt had planned to head back home and get some rest during the two hours he'd have to wait. But he changed his mind, deciding instead to keep an eye on the glowing Mount Vernon. After all, Caitlin and her friends might get together to give him a fatally warm reception. If he kept the virtual mansion under observation, he should be able to spot their preparations.

Long minutes crept by, but nothing happened around the Corrigan mansion.

At last, a muted *bleep*! sounded. Matt had pre-programmed the warning that midnight had arrived.

Just as he started forward, a figure came through the wall – Matt saw an angry Cat Corrigan. Her hands were balled up in the pockets of the loose jeans she wore, and her bright blue eyes sparkled with fury.

'You threatened me!' she accused. 'Who do you think—'

Matt interrupted her. 'What do you think your pal the cowboy was doing with his six-shooter? Or the frog with the sword? Or your large sparkly friend with his great big fists? This isn't a one-way street, Caitlin. You guys asked me for something, and I delivered. Don't think you can blow me off now.'

Cat's defiant act disappeared. Now all that confronted him was a scared kid. 'We'll go see the others. But don't threaten them! They're half over the edge as it is. One push, and they'll do something *really* stupid.'

'Why are they half over the edge?' Matt demanded.

But Caitlin only turned big, fear-filled eyes toward him.

He shrugged. 'Okay, no questions – at least till I'm all the way in.'

Caitlin held out the black skull that would take them to the other virtual vandals. Matt took her hand, hoping the lightless icon wasn't a symbol of things to come.

They hurtled wildly across the Net. Matt wasn't sure, but he thought they bounced along a different route from the one they'd taken the last time.

But their destination seemed the same – the small, featureless white room where the other three members of the group stood waiting for them.

At least they didn't have their weapons out.

Tex the cartoon cowboy tilted back his ten-gallon hat. 'Feller that pushes as hard as you do ought to have something to back it up,' he said ominously.

'Right,' Matt said. 'I wouldn't want to get you *srdit*.'

'Durn tootin',' the cowboy said. 'I rile up real easy.'

Matt allowed himself a small smile. His studying had paid off. '*Srdit*' was the word many Balkan nationalities used for 'angry.' The cowboy's instant recognition showed that he spoke one of those languages.

Gerald Savage shook his big, jeweled fist in Matt's face. 'Give me one reason why I shouldn't squash you like a bloody bug,' he demanded.

'How about honor?' Matt asked. 'You people who are rolling in dough always talk as though you're better than other people, because you have honor. That means you're supposed to pay your debts – *and make good on your promises*.'

'I made no promises—' the big frog began.

'Your loud friend there did,' Matt said. ' "If you want to run with us, you have to show what you can do" – that's pretty much what he said. So I showed you – I got CeeCee into Sean McArdle's veeyar – someplace where your rich-kid connections couldn't get you. And what do I get in the way of thanks? The door slammed in my face.'

He glanced over at the scowling cowboy. 'Not very *faktura*, is it, Tex?'

The cartoon cowboy began to nod, agreeing that it wasn't fair, then stopped. "'Fraid I don't *comprende* what you're sayin' there, amigo.'

Matt decided to go for broke. 'Come off it, Serge. You gave yourself away when I spoke Serbo-Croatian before. I don't think your Idiom Savant program automatically translates all languages.'

He rounded on the other proxied-up kids. 'Then we have the frog swordsman – it must take a pretty warped sense of humor to see yourself that way, Lucien.' Matt twisted the knife a little, thanks to the research he'd done. 'But you prefer to be called Luc, don't you?'

His chest was tight as he confronted the looming, jeweled proxy. 'And you, with your British slang and the loud way you hate the Irish. Who *else* could you be but Gerry the Savage?'

The room was quiet, except for the sound of sharp, sucked-in breath.

Matt had never seen Cat Corrigan's eyes bigger, bluer – or more scared.

He plunged on, before they pulled themselves together and killed him. 'You asked me what I've got to back myself up. I think I just showed you. When I came in, I wasn't sure I'd gotten you all. But it looks like I managed to hit the nail – on each head.'

Matt held up a hand as Gerald Savage lumbered forward. 'I haven't told anybody – *yet*. But there are files out in the Net, ready to be opened if, say, something happened to me.'

The big, jeweled figure turned its anger on Caitlin. 'How did he get it out of you?' he demanded, his voice grating. '*How?*'

'She had nothing to do with it!' Matt shouted. 'I rounded you all up with data searches. It was easy enough – if you knew what to look for.' He spread his arms. 'What more do I need to do to show you that I can pull my weight in this bunch?'

Lucien Valery switched from his frog to his swordsman shape. 'Why should we trust you?' he asked, his lip curling.

'For the best reason of all,' Matt shot back. 'Because now you *have to.*'

He looked at the four unmasked thrill-seekers. 'I gave you everything you asked for – and a bit more, I'd say. You guys think you're something special – well, maybe not.' Matt took a deep breath, still pushing. 'You can be found – so why not face facts and make me a full partner?'

Chapter 11

From his previous meetings, Matt figured there were two possible reactions from the virtual vandals. Either they'd kill him, or they'd cut his connection. Luckily, he guessed right. Even more luckily, they went with reaction number two.

Spangles of neon light spun around Matt with dizzying speed as he tumbled through the Net. His stomach heaved as if he were being whirled about in a high-speed carnival ride. Whoever taught this little trick to those rich kids had a nasty sense of humor. Matt would have been left lost in the Net for hours, after blowing his virtual lunch all over the place. He'd have a hard enough time finding his way home, much less ever tracing where he'd been.

That is, he *should* have had a hard time. Instead, he had a little golden thread in his hands as he slowed down and straightened himself out.

Matt had been expecting to be blown out. That was why he'd worked so hard on the special program he'd worked into the key icon. It had spun the golden thread he could now follow back to the virtual vandals' little clubhouse.

Pulling himself hand over hand, Matt began to retrace his path. The thread was incredibly thin, the barest glimmer of color in his hands. Out in the real world, wire or fishing line this fine would have sliced through his fingers. In the virtual world of the Net, each pull on the line accelerated his speed back to whatever node the rich kids were using.

Still, he was moving more slowly than he had when he and Caitlin had bounced their way in here. Matt could see now that the neon glare of the Web was growing dimmer.

Of course! He thought. Dead storage.

The virtual landscape changed into a vista of regularly spaced mounds with a dim firefly glow. Row after row of them spread out ahead, warehouse units for old records and seldom-used data. Matt couldn't help the morbid thought that the data dumps looked like a cemetery full of freshly dug graves.

Once again, the Genius had shown his or her cleverness, hacking into dormant systems to create a personal chat room that would never be discovered unless someone asked a university library for some obscure study on Arctic butterflies, or tried to chase down some ancient piece of genealogy.

But Matt couldn't hold back a feeling of anger at the selfishness the Genius was showing – the rich kids, too. In creating their little meeting place, who knows what data had been erased?

More importantly, who knew if there were backup copies? That data could be lost forever!

Well, Matt was sure of one thing as he followed the golden thread over the information mausoleums. He'd managed to identify the four vandals. But he still had no legal proof against them. And, unless Serge Woronov turned out to have unexpected computer skills, he still couldn't identify whoever was behind them – the shadowy figure he'd named the Genius.

An unpleasant thought made him stop in his progress. Could the vandals themselves not know who was giving them technical support for their midnight visits? In this world of proxies, the Genius could appear in any face when he dealt with the rich kids.

Then there was no more time to stop and think. The golden thread angled downward, toward one of the dump sites. Matt put on speed. This would be the test of his programming. If he'd done it right, he'd give the virtual vandals the shock of their young lives.

If not, the program would crash and he'd be home with another killer headache.

The low-lying mound rose up in front of him like an artificial hill.

Matt hit it – and went through!

He'd been afraid that the vandals might have left their meeting place while he was gone. But the four kids were still in the white room, arguing at the top of their lungs.

'Why can't we let him help us?' Cat Corrigan pleaded.

'You know bloody well why!' Gerald Savage sounded as if he'd heard Cat's line once too often. D'you think you know who is going to jump up and welcome him with open arms?'

'How odd – you're the one always telling us that you're not afraid of . . . our friend,' Luc Valery sneered.

'And what friend is this?' Matt asked.

Their reactions would have been funny – if they hadn't been so dangerous. Serge's cowboy proxy leapt into the air as if he'd been goosed by an electric eel. But he was also twisting and bringing his huge gun up to aim. Gerald the

Savage looked like a big, jeweled fish as his mouth dropped open. Then he roared with fury and stomped forward, fists raised.

Luc Valery morphed into his swordsman form and unsheathed his blade. Caitlin just stared at him as if she'd seen a ghost – or perhaps a ghost-to-be. 'I told you not to push them,' she said in a hollow voice.

'Okay, I'm completely convinced of how tough you are,' Matt said sarcastically as he faced murderer's row. 'Maybe now you can think of using your heads instead of your fists.'

He stared up at Gerald Savage, who seemed to be the leader – at least he was the most angry. 'I don't know why you get so bent out of shape whenever I show how I can be useful to you people – or did you think you were the only people on earth who could drop system trapdoors behind themselves?'

'You see?' Caitlin cried, as if he were proving her argument. 'He knows this stuff, and we don't. Suppose he could help us?'

'Enough of that!' Gerald Savage cut her off. His voice came out in a deep growl, but at least he wasn't moving to pound Matt . . . yet.

'Sorry, Yank, but the position's taken – by a very dangerous sort of chap – person.'

'Still, it sounds as if you could use me.' Matt turned to the others, pretending he hadn't heard Savage's slip. Now he'd learned two things by coming back. The Genius *wasn't* one of the four kids who actually did the raids. And the Genius was a very dangerous sort of *chap*, as Gerald had been about to say. That meant that the Genius, whoever he was, was male.

That narrows it down to half the population, Matt thought sarcastically. If I stay alive long enough, maybe I'll pick up a few more clues.

'Perhaps we could use someone with your abilities,' Luc Valery said, suddenly taking sides with Caitlin. 'But if the others are afraid . . .'

'I'm not afraid!' Gerald Savage raged. 'And I'll show you! We'll hit the Net right now – and pay a little visit to Sean McArdle's veeyar.'

'B-But we're not supposed to—' a surprised Cat Corrigan began.

Gerald didn't let her finish, drowning her voice out with his.

'Blow all that!' he shouted furiously. 'I want a chance at that jumped-up little Paddy, and I'm going to take it – you follow?'

Luc, still in his swordsman proxy, gave the British boy a thin smile. 'Since you put it so charmingly.'

Serge Woronov's cartoon cowboy tipped back his hat and shrugged. 'If everybody else is going, I reckon I'll come along.'

Gerald whirled his hulking proxy around to loom over Matt. 'You'll come along, too, won't you, Mr Oh-so-clever Yank? Do your bit. Be right there in the thick of it with the rest of us.'

Then he turned to Caitlin, his voice cold and cruel. 'Happy now, luv? We'll see just how much help your new friend can be.'

The Savage thrust out a jeweled hand toward a shelf on the wall. A dozen or so icons lay scattered across it.

'Find yourself a proxy, and we'll get going.'

Cat Corrigan seemed pale as the walls while she selected an icon. Activating the program, she became taller and older – a pale-skinned woman with waist-length black hair and a flowing black gown. Her eyes seemed to gleam from within, and her lips were a shocking shade of red. And when she opened them – she had fangs!

She'd chosen to go as a vampire!

'Excellent choice,' Luc Valery complimented her. Matt noticed that the French boy was staying in his swordsman form.

Luc smiled as he noticed Matt's eyes on him. But it wasn't a friendly expression. 'In my country, the laws are somewhat different from your American Constitution,' the young swordsman said. 'The police are allowed to use *agents provocateurs* – spies who can push people to commit crimes. They get off scot-free, even if they commit that crime as well.'

He ran a practiced hand over the hilt of his sword. 'You didn't push the Savage to go off on this little adventure. But if you try to betray us, then blood will flow for the vampire, eh?'

Matt forced himself to laugh. 'Right. I look like a cop, don't I?'

Luc laughed just as mirthlessly. 'In this world of masks, who knows the truth?'

'If you two are finished with the philosophy, you can join the circle,' Gerald Savage said. The others had already gathered around him.

Matt noticed that the English boy had somehow shrunk his jeweled proxy. He wasn't a giant anymore, just a large human – say, about the size of a high-school football linebacker. In his palm, Savage held an icon whose glow clashed with his bejeweled glitter. It was in the shape of an arrow, and it gave off a poisonous green radiance that reflected off Gerald's gemstone hands. As they stood around him, everyone's faces were speckled with mirrored pinpoints of sickly green – as if they'd all caught some terrible disease.

'Link up,' the Savage commanded.

Matt glanced around. If he didn't go along, the vandals might well jump him. And even worse, he'd blow his chance to get in solidly with them and perhaps discover the mastermind who was pulling their strings.

He took a deep breath. 'Count me in.'

Caitlin grabbed Matt's left hand, clutching tightly. Luc took his right.

The green glow blazed up as if the little icon were truly on fire. Luc and Serge each seized one of Gerald's elbows. The room faded around them, and all of a sudden, they were rocketing across the Net.

Matt had half-expected them to shoot across the sky like a vast green comet. But apparently they were stealthed. They seemed to give off no light, and the neon glare of the virtual constructs all around their flight path didn't reflect off them, either. Not even Savage's jeweled body caught any gleams from the blazing collections of computer imagery they passed.

The area began to look familiar, and Matt realized they were approaching the modernistic virtual office tower that housed the Irish embassy's bit of cyberspace.

As they came up to the glowing wall, Matt had a sudden unwelcome thought. What if Captain Winters and Net

Force had warned embassy security about the trapdoor they'd discovered in the copy of Sean's veeyar programming? They could be flying right into a trap!

Well, he thought, I guess this would finally convince the captain that there's a diplomatic connection to this vandalism. After he gets over his stroke about me being along.

It might end up with Cat and her friends getting nailed for their lawless activities.

But would the Genius be able to recruit a new bunch of bored kids to keep the vandalism going?

Too late to worry now. They approached the wall of light – and flashed right through. A couple of seconds' routing along the system and they arrived in Sean McArdle's veeyar. The space was just as large as it had been at his press conference. But now the cavernous space had been turned into a library.

Matt looked around in amazement. A high arched ceiling was held up by two-story-tall carved wooden bookcases. There were just too many details for this to be made up. Sean must have based the veeyar on a real location – maybe someplace famous in Ireland.

Then Matt saw the ornate wooden desk at the far end of the big room – with a surprised-looking Sean McArdle behind it.

'What—?' he began.

'Trash the place!' Gerald Savage commanded, charging straight for the Irish boy.

Whooping like savages on the warpath, Luc and Serge set to work. Luc's long, thin blade seemed more like a wrecking bar or a buzz-saw as he sliced through the delicate wood carvings. Serge unholstered his cartoon six-gun and started blasting away. From the holes it was making, the silly-looking weapon must have been loaded either with buckshot or small mortar shells. And it had the typical cartoon-gun's capacity. Matt counted Serge squeezing off fourteen shots without having to reload.

The boys managed to cut through one of the graceful pillars supporting the weight of the bookshelves above. The small walkway began to sag.

'Here it comes!' Luc shouted gleefully. He and Serge scampered out of the way as an entire portion of the huge bookcase gave way, crashing down and spilling volumes across the floor.

'Gather 'em up!' Serge called to Matt and Caitlin. 'Pile 'em, while we find something to make a real campfire!'

But neither Matt nor the girl moved toward the books. Both whirled as they heard a cry of pain from behind them.

Gerry Savage had reached the desk – and Sean McArdle. The Irish boy was wobbling on his feet beyond the beautiful wooden construct. He was blinking his eyes and cradling the side of his face.

Even from a distance, Matt could see the large, red hand-print on Sean's cheek.

The Savage, however, was ignoring Sean just for the moment. He swept a glittering arm across the desktop, disrupting the ordered ranks of icons – Matt had never seen so many for a single computer. Program markers tumbled to the floor, and the Savage ground them under his feet.

'You bog-trotting baboons think you can run the world because you know *computers*.' Savage made the last word sound like an obscenity. 'Strutting around as if you were the best of the earth – when you're nothing but a bunch of traitors to the Crown!'

Sean might have been hurt and scared, but he still answered. 'We were saddled with England for eight hundred years, to be beaten, starved, and treated like animals. We've been free little more than a hundred years – and we're doing quite well without your moth-eaten Crown, thank you.'

With a wordless roar, Savage hurled the desk aside. It toppled and shattered. Then he started advancing on Sean McArdle.

Matt raced down the length of the half-ruined library as fast as his legs would take him. Sean was tall, but built like a stringbean. The massive Gerry Savage could take him apart.

And they know how to hurt people in veeyar, Matt suddenly thought in horror.

Savage was still only slapping Sean around when Matt reached them. But the Irish boy couldn't even defend himself. He was wobbling on his feet.

And when he went down, Savage pounced, his hands going for a stranglehold.

'Are you crazy?' Matt demanded, trying to haul Savage off.

For a reply, Savage merely swept a heavy arm into Matt's chest.

It felt like being hit by a pebble-studded wrecking ball. He stumbled backwards, trying to breathe.

Soft hands caught Matt. It was Cat Corrigan.

'You've got to do something!' The face of her vampiress proxy was a mask of terror. 'He's going to kill that boy!'

Chapter 12

What do you think *I* can do? A frantic voice screeched inside Matt's skull. Savage has all the advantages in a fight. He's bigger, stronger, and he can hurt people in veeyar. I can't.

Hurt people... The mental words seemed to echo as Matt grabbed Caitlin by the arms. 'I'll try,' he said, 'but you've got to help me.'

'Help?' Cat was almost babbling. 'How?'

'Give me a hand.' Matt went to the wreckage of Sean McArdle's virtual desk, hauling out a large, splintered slab of wood. Caitlin joined him as he dragged it to where Gerald Savage was singlemindedly strangling the Irish ambassador's son.

'Okay,' Matt panted. 'I'm letting go. You make this fall on Savage, then jump on it.'

'Me?'

'*You* can hurt him – I can't,' Matt yelled. 'Now just do it!'

He released the piece of wreckage. For a second it wobbled, then Caitlin threw her weight against it. The heavy wooden desk fragment seemed to fall in slow motion. But Gerald the Savage didn't even seem to be aware of it – until it landed across his back.

Savage felt the impact, even through his jewel-tough skin. He screamed in pain, then screamed again as Caitlin leapt onto the piece of wreckage now pinning him.

Grunting, Savage levered himself around. One good heave freed him from the wooden wreckage – and sent Caitlin flying.

Matt managed to catch her and keep her on her feet. But his eyes were focused beyond Savage, on Sean McArdle. The Irish boy scrambled up, one hand on his throat. The instant he realized he was free, he vanished from the veeyar.

Turning to resume his unfinished business, the Savage made the kind of noise lions do after being cheated out of a kill. 'You let him get away!' he screamed, his voice thick with bloodlust.

Fists clenched, he advanced on Matt and Caitlin.

'Trashing a veeyar is one thing,' Matt shouted. 'Killing someone is another!'

'However it happened, he's out now,' Luc Valery said. He and Serge had finally stopped their vandalism at Savage's scream and run to join the others. 'Security will be here any second.'

Serge didn't even comment on that. His cartoon-cowboy proxy was simply gone, like a blown-out candle flame.

The thought of consequences finally penetrated Savage's fury. 'Right,' he finally said. Then he jutted a finger at Matt. 'But I'm not done with you.'

The British boy vanished, then Luc winked out.

Cat grabbed Matt's hand. 'Let's get out of here.'

He let Caitlin do the piloting, wondering if they'd wind

up back at Bradford's chem lab again. Instead, they popped up in another library.

'Library of Congress,' Cat explained. 'Even at this time of night – or morning, they get a lot of queries.'

'Saves on the phone bill,' Matt said.

They bounced through a series of heavily trafficked Net nodes until they arrived at last at Casa Corrigan.

Matt noticed, however, that Cat landed them on the virtual lawn outside the replica of Mount Vernon, not in her own veeyar. Somewhere along the way, she'd shed her Madame Dracula proxy. It was a teenaged girl who faced him – pretty, disheveled . . . and very scared.

'Thanks for doing what you did,' Caitlin said. 'I couldn't even think – and there was no way I could have moved that chunk of wood by myself.' She shuddered. 'The Savage really lost it this time. I was afraid he was going to squish that guy like an overripe tomato.'

'Look, Savage isn't the boss of this gang, is he?' Matt asked.

Caitlin shook her head. 'He's just the biggest of us – and the loudest.'

'I wouldn't think he had the brains to find his way out of a paper bag – unless he tore it.' Matt gave the girl a long, hard look. 'And, from the way he talks about computers, he doesn't have the programming smarts to create the bag of tricks you guys have been using. But then, we already know about that. Savage blabbed about him – it had to be a him, didn't it? Old Gerald called him a "dangerous sort of chap" before he realized what he was doing.'

He looked into Caitlin's eyes. 'The big brain is also your boss, isn't he, Cat? The one who really calls the shots.'

'Sometimes,' Caitlin admitted. 'We get a bunch of labels – trapdoors. Some we're supposed to drop on certain kids or places. The rest are for us to use any way we like.'

'So you visit them later and trash 'em.'

She shook her head. 'Some we're not supposed to. The Irish kid – McArdle – we weren't supposed to go back there.'

'And that thing in the baseball stadium . . . that wasn't just a trapdoor.'

'When he told us – when I first heard, I thought it would be a joke. Just shooting down a bunch of simulated baseball players, right?' Caitlin looked sick. 'But then, people in the stands began falling. I never realized how many people came to those games in holo.'

'So is this "he" you're talking about as dangerous as Savage says?' Matt asked. 'If he is, why don't you just bail out?'

His questions seemed to snap Caitlin out of her cooperative mood. 'Yes, he is,' she replied, both angry and scared. Then she sounded sad. 'And, no, I can't.'

A second later, she'd disappeared inside the imitation Mount Vernon.

Matt knew better than to try following her. If the security systems didn't get him, the systems crash would. And if he was going to end up back home, he might as well get there without a pounding headache.

He bounced out of the Corrigans' virtual estate. Moments later, Matt opened his eyes, back in his own room. But he didn't get out of his computer-link chair. He just sat there, his chin resting on his clasped hands.

He'd done a couple of good things this night – identifying

the virtual vandals, shaking them up, and learning a little bit about the still shadowy figure who provided their technology – and their orders. On the minus side, he hadn't found out about the programming trick that allowed the vandals to hurt people in the veeyar. He'd let himself be pressured into going along on a trashing expedition where a victim had almost gotten killed.

Okay, Matt thought, by being there, I probably managed to save Sean McArdle. But if I hadn't pushed Gerry the Savage, we might never have ended up hacking into that virtual consulate in the first place.

Last and most worrying, he'd turned himself into a definite blip on the Genius' enemy-detection scanners. Before, he'd just been a wannabe trying to find a place with the in-crowd. Now, however, he'd definitely rocked the boat, identifying the vandals, causing Gerry Savage to disobey the Genius' orders. And he'd seen the vandals in action.

None of those things would make the Genius very happy. And the Genius, to quote the words of a big and nasty bully, was 'a dangerous sort of chap.'

Dangerous, and full of computer smarts, Matt thought, scowling. It's definitely time for me to retreat to my secret identity – Matt Hunter, everyday old student.

It was hard enough being an everyday student with only a couple of hours' worth of sleep. Matt dragged himself through his morning classes. He was lucky that his first after-lunch time slot was a library period.

Even so, he was yawning as he began to go over some of the historical material Sandy Braxton had given him. The two officers they were researching, Armistead and Hancock, had served together on several posts out West before the Civil War had started. When the fighting began, they had quickly risen to responsible commands.

Matt began to show a little interest as he kept reading. He was fascinated to see how different leadership was during the Civil War. Officers, even generals, led charges from the front ranks rather than managing their troops from the rear.

Or hiding completely, like the Genius, while others took all the risks.

But a hundred and seventy years ago, officers believed that their men had to be inspired. It was an idea from centuries earlier, when smooth-bore muskets couldn't be aimed more than ninety yards. But in the Civil War, the troops were firing rifles accurate to 660 yards. Gallant gestures by officers also turned them into targets.

Brigadier Armistead had tried a morale-boosting measure on the fatal day of July third, 1863. He'd placed his officer's hat on the tip of his sword, holding it high over his head so his troops would know where 'the old man' was. Certainly, his men had kept following, even though they'd taken horrifying casualties. Only a handful had made it to the top of Cemetery Ridge, and they'd faced point-blank fire. Armistead had gone down, still at the front of the attack.

At least Matt was awake for the rest of the day. But he was fading again as he headed for home on the autobus. His folks weren't home, so he hit the rack for a couple of hours. He was up in time for dinner, although his father couldn't help teasing him a little.

'In my day, we'd be up late at night hitting the books.

What do you call it when you're plugged into your computer until two in the morning?'

'Could be worse,' Mom said with a smile. 'He might have been sitting on front of an old-fashioned computer monitor all that time.'

'I remember that,' Dad laughed. 'We'd call it "getting a CRT tan" – computer nerds used to turn that delicate shade of green.'

Matt just kept his eyes on his plate, shoving the food in. He cleaned the plates and finally headed back up to his room.

Better start hitting some of that classwork, he told himself.

Sinking into the upholstery of his computer-link chair, he began to tune his implants to the receptor equipment in the headrest. A high-pitched buzzing rose in his ears as he closed his eyes.

When he opened them, he was in his personal veeyar, facing the familiar starry sky with the marble slab floating in midair. A second later, though, he faced a very unexpected addition.

Caitlin Corrigan popped into existence, lying across the marble slab like a swimsuit model, one elbow cocked so she could rest her head on her hand.

'Better close your mouth, Matt,' she teased. 'Unless you're trying to catch virtual flies.'

He did his best to make a comeback. 'It – it's just that I don't recall leaving an icon quite so large on my workspace.'

'You were using enough of them last night,' she giggled, toying with the icons across the slab. 'This is your Mr Sticks proxy, your telecommunications program, and the awful things you did to my friendly little protocol.' Cat's eyebrows rose as she poked at her altered earring.

Matt wished for a proxy right now. He just hoped his face wasn't giving away his total shock at Caitlin's familiarity with his personal veeyar. She must have been in and around his veeyar for a while, to figure out all the programs he had set out.

She kept her covergirl pose, even though she was wearing an old sweater and beat-up jeans. 'I don't know why you're so surprised to see me. You did just about challenge us to track you down.'

Then she shook her head, trying to sound stern but somehow coming across as flirty. 'For a whiz, I thought you'd be a lot more serious about using your computer. It's been how long since we got out of school? And you haven't even logged in! Not even a voice command! I'd hate to tell you how long I've been sitting around, waiting for you to turn up.'

'Not all of that time in my computer, I hope,' Matt said, still trying to come to grips with this bolt from the blue.

Cat wagged a finger at him. 'Don't think the whole world revolves around you,' she scolded with a grin. 'I had a couple of other things to do.'

She cocked her head, twirling the ends of her hair around one finger. 'You know, I really wondered what you looked like behind that stick proxy.' Caitlin's grin grew wider. 'I'm glad it's you, even though I have to say I'm surprised.'

'Surprised?' Matt echoed.

She shrugged, swinging up so that she was sitting on the slab. Her hands clasped over her right knee, while her left foot dangled off into the star-filled void.

'I always thought you were one of the good boys,' she said, her voice becoming even more flirtatious.

'Oh, you mean, poor but honest?' Matt teased back.

The girl giggled, nodding her head. 'You got it! I never thought an upstanding junior citizen like you would ever want to hang with us naughty rich kids.'

Matt remembered a line Leif Anderson had used about the wealthy and bored. 'Skill and sneakiness can beat mere money any day.'

Cat laughed, but Matt noticed that her pose was suddenly a lot more tense.

What did I say? he wondered. *Why is she worried all of a sudden?*

Then it hit him. It wasn't Caitlin's computer skill that allowed her to find him. Her sudden appearance – and her flirty act, too – were probably a setup to distract him.

But Matt's thoughtless words had cut through her little act. They'd reminded her of someone else who skill and sneakiness had left him dominating the rich kids of the virtual vandals.

It's the Genius who tracked you down, a cold voice whispered in his skull. *Now he knows who you are.*

A chill ran down his back, but he did his best to keep up the byplay with Caitlin.

'I hope you think this little visit was worthwhile. I mean, it must have taken you a lot of effort.'

Cat relaxed a little, until she caught the barbed hook hidden in the last four words. Her breath caught a little, and for just a second, he could see the fear in her eyes.

'Enjoy it while you can,' she said lightly. 'If I see you tomorrow in school, I'll have to pretend I don't know you.'

She leaned forward. 'Remember, none of us are supposed to be meeting . . . out there.'

She made a little gesture, indicating something beyond the starry skies of Matt's veeyar – the real world.

' "In the flesh" was the way you put it last time,' Matt reminded her. 'Does this mean I've finally become a member of the team?'

Cat still kept her sexy pose, but her eyes grew sharper. 'I couldn't tell you that – but better safe than sorry.'

'Okay,' Matt sighed. 'I guess I'll have to get used to being just another Dexter.'

For a second, he shocked a genuine smile out of Caitlin. But her eyes were still intent as her finger went back to twirling her hair. ''Fraid so. Till I see you again . . .'

She vanished – but just before she did, something dropped among the icons on the marble slab.

Cat Corrigan had left him another earring.

Chapter 13

For long minutes after Cat Corrigan cut out of his veeyar, Matt simply sat still, shattered bits of thoughts running through his mind. Outwardly, he paid no attention at all to the earring lying on his workspace. Had Cat's visit been even more of a setup than he thought? Had the Genius not only used her to distract Matt from who had tracked him down – but also to create a trap?

By picking up that earring, Matt could be setting off any kind of program.

The Genius knows how to hurt people in veeyar, the warning echoed through Matt's confusion. Touching that icon was about as safe as pulling the pin from a live grenade.

But . . .

Cat hadn't looked like a girl about to let someone get blown up. He'd seen through her flirting to recognize who was behind her. Wouldn't he have seen if she meant to do him in?

Right, he told himself sarcastically. *You know all about how pretty, rich girls react when they're backed into a corner.*

But . . .

Cat hadn't wanted Gerry Savage to kill Sean McArdle.

She'd begged Matt to stop him – and more importantly, she'd helped Matt get Savage off the other boy.

Sure, his interior arguer replied. She also sprayed Camden Yards with virtual machine-gun bullets – hitting Leif.

Yes, she'd admitted doing that – but she'd also said she hadn't realized how many people were there in holo, vulnerable to her virtual bullets.

The earring could be a trick, a death-trap . . . or a message. Matt had to find out.

But the first thing he did was cut his computer connection. Jumping out of the computer-link chair, he headed down the hall. His parents were in the living room, watching a holo-drama – something about cops and robbers.

'Something up, son?' Mr Hunter asked.

Matt shook his head. 'Nope. Just wanted to stretch a little.'

He went back to his room, opened the window, and slipped out.

Good thing I've got a separate farecard with some money on it, he thought.

Maybe he was being completely paranoid. A telephone call could have gotten what he needed – even a quick telecommunications visit through the Net.

But Matt wasn't about to trust himself to the webwork of circuitry most people used. Not after someone had invaded his personal system, sending Cat Corrigan into his own veeyar. Matt always thought he had pretty good security for his computer – not the megabucks type that rich people could surround themselves with, or the heavy-duty government programs that Net Force used.

Against the Genius, though, his security had been about as strong as wet toilet paper. Before Matt could use his system again, he wanted to check for bugs, tracers, trap-doors, and tricks.

Since the Genius knew who Matt was, he could tap the Hunters' phone as well as Matt's computer. He might even be able to snag Matt's credit-card transactions out of computer systems.

Matt might indeed simply be paranoid about a guy who seemed to be working on a bargain-store antique. But he couldn't be *sure* what the Genius had in the way of resources – or what tricks his opponent might have up his sleeve.

No, Matt thought as he walked from the Metro station to the building where David Gray lived. It's better – safer – to do this face-to-face.

Luckily, David was the one who answered when Matt buzzed from the downstairs lobby. 'David? It's Matt. I've got trouble, and I hope you can help me.'

'Come on up,' David replied.

Matt was ready the moment David opened his apartment door. 'The guy behind the virtual vandals got into my computer,' he whispered.

'Sure, Matt,' David said loudly. 'It's in my room.' He led the way into the living room, where Mrs Gray was watching a hologram comedy. 'Hello, Matt,' she said.

'Matt needs something for school,' David said. 'It will only take a minute.'

As they headed down the hallway, David spoke in a lower voice. 'You're lucky my dad is working the night shift this month, so you've only got my mom to deal with.' David's father was a detective on the D.C. police force. 'Dad would have taken you to interrogation city, wanting to know why we couldn't do whatever it was in veeyar.' He grinned. 'Plus, it's her favorite show – *Old Friends*.'

They reached the room which David shared with his two younger brothers, Tommy and James. Even with bunkbeds, the place always seemed crowded – the kids' toys fighting for space with David's computer. Right now, the younger boys were playing a loud shoot-em-up game on part of David's system.

'Out!' David said, pointing to the door. 'We need the computer for a little while.'

'Awwwww!' ten-year-old Tommy complained. 'Right when I finally got to the next level!'

'Computer!' David ordered. 'Game override. Save present simulation. Store as TOMMYTOPSCORE dot GAME.'

The bright holographic image that the boys had been playing on dimmed away. 'Game saved,' the computer announced.

'Hey!' Tommy said. 'I didn't know you could do that!'

'*You* can't,' David told his youngest brother. '*I* can. You can come back and finish when we're done.'

'I'll be out of the grove by then,' Tommy mourned as he and James trooped out the door.

'That game will always start right where you ended,' David promised. He shut the door, then glanced at Matt. 'I don't know why you don't just go to Captain Winters and let the Net Force heavy-duty techs into the system,' he said.

David was a friend, but even so, Matt didn't want to tell

him about the invasion of Sean McArdle's veeyar – and the attack he'd barely managed to stop. After all, David's father was in the police force.

'It's getting very weird,' was all he finally said. 'There may be a clue in my veeyar, but I don't want to pick it up if the boss bad guy is able to see what I'm doing.'

'I don't see how I can help—' David began.

'Your virtual explorer,' Matt interrupted. 'With all the scanning stuff you've got in there, I figure you'd be able to check out my system from here.'

Most boys Matt knew liked to design cool stuff on their computers. Matt had a couple of fantasy race cars that he designed, tinkered with, and even took out on fantasy drives. David, however, had a different hobby. He developed spacecraft and exploring modules that worked as well as anything NASA had come up with – at least in veeyar.

David looked a little surprised. 'I hadn't thought of that,' he said. 'But you're right. We can set it to look for emission sources and unexpected energy concentrations, and work from there.'

He opened a package of datascrips and inserted a blank into his computer. 'I'll make a copy of the probe first, just so we'll know if it gets tampered with while it's in your system.'

He gave a series of orders to his computer, then turned to Matt with a grin. 'Want to see how your veeyar looks from outside?'

'I think you'd be better off if you just went by telemetry,' Matt warned.

David frowned. 'It'll be a lot more clumsy,' he objected.

'This guy makes bad things happen to people in veeyar,'

Matt said. 'If he's set up something nasty in my system, I don't mind risking your probe. You've got a copy right there.' He pointed to the datascrip on the computer desk. 'But we stay as far away as possible.'

'I guess you've got a point,' David admitted. He gave more orders to the computer, calling up all sorts of security subroutines.

David gave Matt another grin. 'When you've got two nosy kid brothers, you learn how to keep things under wraps,' he said. A few more orders set up holographic scales and gauges for the probe's reports.

'In we go,' David said, authorizing the telecommunications link.

Matt stared at the gauges, but they told him nothing.

'The good news,' David told him, 'is that nothing's happened. Your veeyar hasn't been nuked or anything.'

He pointed at a gauge. 'But there are several outward energy leaks that wouldn't occur in your garden-variety veeyar.'

'So it is bugged,' Matt said.

'Your guess was right.' David gave some orders to the probe. 'Let's see if we can get a better look—'

He broke off, pointing at another gauge. 'Whoa! Self-destruct! Not enough to hurt, even if you'd been in the veeyar. I think this guy just doesn't want people checking out his work.'

They spent some more time cleaning out a couple more of the Genius' toys, including the Trojan horse program that had allowed Caitlin Corrigan to come inside – and leave these little souvenirs behind.

'Only one more out-of-place item left,' David reported.

'There's an alien icon on your work surface – a program that doesn't belong.'

'That's the clue I was talking about,' Matt said. 'Can your probe trigger it?'

David gave orders. A few seconds later, he shrugged. 'Looks like a ten-second voice clip. A message for you, maybe.'

He continued to give Matt an odd look. 'At least nothing blew up, buddy.'

Half an hour later, Matt felt a little foolish climbing back through the window into his room.

Better safe than sorry, he told himself.

Stepping into the hallway, Matt went to the kitchen to get a glass of milk.

'Still working?' his father asked.

'Just about done, I hope,' Matt replied. He went back to his room and picked up the datascrip with everything he knew about felt the virtual vandals. Stepping to the door, he put it down in the hall. Then he went back inside and began giving orders to his computer. A scale model of his veeyar appeared over his desk. Matt moved over behind his bed, the only thing available to duck behind . . . just in case. Then he gave the order to trigger Cat Corrigan's earring icon.

'Matt, I've got to see you.' Caitlin's voice came through a little tinny from the reduced-scale model. 'It has to be in the flesh. No computers, no phones . . . no holograms – and soon.'

Even with the substandard voice reproduction, she sounded scared.

Matt stood very still, looking at his carefully constructed veeyar. Then he ordered his computer to erase the whole thing. Not just to delete the file, but to destroy all records of his workspace – and everything that had happened in there.

The next morning, Matt took an earlier autobus to school. He knew that Cat Corrigan usually drove in, and she did this morning. Matt had to laugh to himself. He wondered if he'd stand out, changing his schedule. But Cat was much more attention-getting, swooping in to park in a classic Copperhead.

Matt knew his cars. This thing had to be a good thirty years old. But it was fast – faster than almost anything out there. And, he had to admit, it had style. But it didn't seem exactly in character for Cat.

Well, one thing she did was distract anyone's attention from Matt. But she also attracted about every car-crazy guy in the school. Matt had hoped for a couple of quick words before Prep Period.

Instead, he wound up standing at the edge of an admiring crowd.

The whole class schedule seemed perversely set up to keep them from even bumping into one another. If Matt saw Caitlin in the mad dash between classes, it was usually at the far end of a hallway, heading in the opposite direction from where he had to go.

He was hoping for a chance to catch up with her in the lunchroom, but as she came in, so did Sandy Braxton. 'Hey, Matt! Great news! My father has some friends who are into battle re-enactments.'

In his research Matt had read about organizations where

people got together, dressed in Civil War uniforms and pretended to re-fight old battles. Since northern Virginia had seen major campaigns during the war, it wouldn't be surprising that several of these clubs might exist in the Washington area.

At another time, he would have been more interested to hear what Sandy had to say.

Instead, Matt was wishing the floor would open up under the idiot. He was blocking the way to Cat Corrigan.

'Anyway, they've got holos of their battles. They were actually up in Pennsylvania, and did a re-enactment of Pickett's Charge.'

'Um,' Matt said brilliantly, trying to step around. Caitlin was walking right by!

She was carrying a portfolio full of datascrips and written notes. As she passed, a piece of paper slid loose.

A note?

Matt moved for it, but Sandy scooped up the paper in midair.

'Hey, Caitlin! You lost this!'

Cat turned and gave Matt an annoyed, 'get-with-the-program!' sort of look.

Sandy handed over the sheet, reading it. 'A classical guitar concert! Who goes to those things?'

She rolled her eyes, every inch a Leet. 'Oh, I know! I fouled up the printing menu on my computer, and this came out.'

As Cat spoke, she crumpled up the paper. But she gave Matt a sharp look.

Matt watched the balled-up wad fly into a garbage bin. He headed over that way, finally managing to get rid of Sandy Braxton.

He was in luck, retrieving the note before somebody dumped a tray of chilli con mystery meat over it.

Throughout lunch, the little wad of paper seemed to weigh in his pocket as if it were made of lead. Matt walked over to a tree, leaned back against the trunk, and unscrunched the paper.

One side was a poster from the school's music club, announcing a classical guitar recital for that afternoon.

The other side was empty.

Matt frowned. Was it a code? Could there be secret writing? He remembered reading something as a kid about lemon juice . . .

He rested his head against the rough bark. No, the message was right in front of him. What better place to meet? The recital would take place in the auditorium, a large, dark room. And classical guitars wouldn't need electronic or computer enhancement. Just old-fashioned fingers, old-fashioned ears – perfect!

Matt arrived at the auditorium out of breach and slightly late. He slipped through the doors, standing in the rear of the seats, trying to let his eyes adjust. A serious girl sat on a chair in a pool of light, her fingers flying as a complicated rhythm filled the air.

Where was Caitlin?

The music ended, and golden hair suddenly flashed before Matt's eyes as Caitlin rose from a back-row seat. She applauded, and as the girl left the stage, Caitlin brushed past Matt.

A deft hand tucked another note into his shirt pocket. Then, without even seeming to see him, Caitlin left the auditorium.

Matt sank into a seat, crossing his arms across his chest – and slipping out the note. He waited impatiently for the next piece of music to end – under the circumstances it seemed to take forever – and then left the auditorium, too.

He walked to his locker, opened the door, and spread the note on top of his books. It simply said:

SHERIDAN CIRCLE
3:30

He knew the place – it was one of the many traffic circles spread around Washington. It was a bit of a walk from Bradford. He checked his watch. He'd better move if he was supposed to be there by three-thirty!

Matt reached Sheridan Circle with about half a minute to spare. He glanced around the wealthy neighborhood. Quite a few countries had their embassies in this area. If one of the virtual vandals should spot him . . .

A second later, Matt knew why Caitlin had driven the Copperhead to school. The unmistakable shape of the classic car came whipping around the traffic circle. Caitlin pulled up, Matt jumped aboard, and they whizzed round the rest of the circle and across the Buffalo Bridge into Georgetown.

The girl was silent as she piloted the car through the local streets and then onto an expressway.

'Well?' Matt said. 'I thought you wanted to talk.'

'We – the guys and I – are only supposed to meet through the Net. It's supposed to be for protection – if nobody sees us together, we can't be connected.' She glanced at Matt. 'But I'm beginning to think it's more of a control thing.'

'So you wanted to break the rules, and you chose me because I can't tell on you – I don't know who to tell.'

Cat's teeth sank into her lower lip. 'I – I wanted to explain some things. Maybe you look at us and think we have it made – the rich kids, living a glamorous life. Let me tell you something. After your tenth diplomatic party, they all start looking alike. You get . . . I guess the word is *bored*.'

Her eyes were on the traffic ahead as she went on. 'It's not like we have families. My dad has been running for something as long as I can remember. I barely see him or Mom. Luc – I something think his jokes are a way to get his parents to admit he's alive. Gerald is over here because he got thrown out of most of the boarding schools in England. And Serge – he hates his father for getting into politics. It made him an ambassador, but it got his mother killed in the last round of troubles in the Balkans.'

'Poor little rich kids, huh?' Matt said.

'Make that *dumb* little rich kids,' Cat said bitterly. 'Bored, angry, and suddenly we have a chance to act out our fantasies, like something in a comic book. Secret identities and everything.'

'Except you weren't superheroes, but villains.'

'Get over it! We trashed a couple of veeyars. Anybody with a brain has a backup on datascrip. Kids with spraypaint did more actual damage than we did.'

'And the people who got hurt?'

She sank a little in her seat. 'That's the dark side of the fantasy.' She glanced again at Matt, pleading with him to understand. 'When you're rich and pretty, lots of people want to do favors for you. I never saw the hook in this – and neither did the others. Serge and the Savage were amazed when they discovered they could deck people in veeyar – frankly, they got carried away.'

'You don't have to tell me. I saw what Savage did to Sean McArdle.'

'That's not the real Gerry. He's lashing out with his fists because that's all he knows about fighting the trap we're caught in.'

'Trap?' Matt echoed.

'The person who set up our little game also set *us* up. We're being blackmailed, Matt. For every trapdoor we leave behind to go visiting, we set two more that we're not allowed to use.'

'What do you mean allowed?'

Caitlin's voice grew tight. '*Ordered* would be a better word. I don't know what those trapdoors are being used for, but Gerry broke a major rule when he took us into Sean McArdle's veeyar.'

They were coming up on an exit near Matt's house. Caitlin shifted lanes and pulled onto the exit ramp. She drove a couple of blocks, then stopped the car. 'I told you all this because you're not in too deeply yet. You can still walk away. Just go home and forget we ever existed.'

'Maybe I could help you,' Matt said. 'Do you know who's giving the orders?'

Caitlin pointed to the door. 'Just go home, Matt. And be careful.'

Matt was only picking at dinner that evening.

'Isn't your Net Force Explorers meeting tonight?' his mother asked as they finished.

Matt nodded. The Explorers held a virtual meeting every

month, either at regional Net nodes or the much larger chat room in the Net Force Washington computer. Matt really wasn't in the mood to go ... then he thought about the Genius. If that shadowy figure was checking on him, the last place he wanted to be tracked was going to Net Force.

'I don't think I'll be going, Mom,' he said.

'Too tired?' his father asked. 'Maybe you took on too much, helping your classmate with that project.'

'No, that's okay,' Matt said, taking the dishes into the kitchen.

The doorbell rang, and a second later, his father appeared, a half-smile on his face. 'A visitor for you,' he said. 'I figured you'd want to get the suds off your hands. It's a young lady.'

Puzzled, Matt went to the front hall ... to find Cat Corrigan chatting with his mother.

'I hope you don't mind me dropping in like this,' Cat said.

'N-no,' Matt replied. 'Want to go for a walk?'

'Fine.'

'Not too late,' Matt's mother cautioned.

As they walked away from the house, Caitlin's polite young visitor act disintegrated. Her eyes were frantic as they walked down the street. 'You said you wanted to help. I don't know what you can do – what anyone can do.'

'About what?' Matt said.

'Gerry,' Caitlin answered in a hoarse voice. 'He's dead. Hit and run, about half an hour ago.'

Chapter 14

Matt stared in shock. 'Could it have been an accident?'

The moment the words were out of his lips, he knew the answer, and said as much. 'No, this was no coincidence.'

'Not unless poor Gerry was the kind to have bad luck and poor timing,' Caitlin agreed.

'It's just that I would have expected some kind of virtual revenge,' Matt said. 'Running somebody down with a car – that's pretty cold.' He glanced at Caitlin. 'And pretty final.'

'I know.' Caitlin shuddered. 'I thought maybe he'd get a warning, or some kind of punishment.'

'I guess this guy never trained dogs,' Matt muttered.

Caitlin turned to him. 'What?'

'It's a line my uncle used to use. If you're training a puppy and he piddles on the carpet, you don't shoot him – that just wastes all the training that's gone before.'

'But there are other puppies,' Caitlin said harshly. 'Four of us, including you. Maybe Gerry made himself expendable right when a possible replacement came along. Or,' she choked, 'maybe we've *all* become expendable.'

Matt didn't like the sound of that. 'Whatever's going on, it's certainly gotten my attention,' he said. 'But I need to know what's happened before I can start to figure out what's happening. Who's pulling the strings on all this?'

Caitlin let out a long sigh. 'All right, I'll tell you. It's a guy who used to go to school with us. Maybe you remember him – Rob Falk.'

Matt frowned. He had a fuzzy image of a tall, gangly kid, a sort of super-Dexter. High-water pants, pocket protector, wild hair always standing up in a cowlick, always working with the computers. Falk hadn't been around in a while. Did he drop out or leave? There was something . . . Matt tried to reach for an elusive memory as Caitlin went on.

'Rob was – well, a nerd. He used to call himself a nerd to the Nth power. But he got me through bonehead computing, so he was useful. At the time, I thought he might have had a crush on me.'

Caitlin laughed without any trace of humor. 'To make a long story short, he did some work inside my system. What I didn't know at the time was that he'd left a trapdoor. Then, some time after he left Bradford, I found some program icons in my veeyar. There were some proxies, and a program that let me into all sorts of places through trapdoors. One day, after I'd scared the fertilizer out of one of my snooty classmates by turning her romance sim into a horror story, I came back to my system to find Rob waiting for me.

'He knew I'd been using his programs, and he had more to offer.' Caitlin shook her head. 'It sounded so cool – getting together some kids who could be trusted, dropping trapdoors by day, coming back in disguise by night . . . I even helped recruit the guys. Gerry I just asked. Luc and Serge, I planted trapdoors in their computers. They thought it was funny. So did I, at first.'

'Then it began to change?'

She nodded. 'Rob had all these virtual tools, stuff you couldn't buy. Incredible proxies. Sneaky ways into all kinds of systems. That program to make people feel a virtual punch. But he had chores for us, too. Places we had to go and drop trapdoors. At first it was easy – we could take care of our assignments at virtual parties. But he kept getting more and more demanding. He'd been on our case about McArdle for a couple of weeks.'

'What about the baseball game?'

'That was Gerry's idea. He was getting a little antsy about being ordered around by a guy he considered a pipsqueak.'

Looks like the pipsqueak finally took him out, Matt thought. But he didn't say anything as Caitlin went on.

'The Savage always hated baseball. He thought it would be a hoot to disrupt a major-league game. Rob went along to keep Gerry cooperative, even though it took a lot of special programming.' She looked even sadder. 'Sometimes I think it was the Savage's way of yelling for help – a very public commotion to get people's attention. After that, though, things really began coming apart. Shooting those people – it upset me. But it just made the guys worse. And . . . well, you know the rest.'

Yeah, Matt thought, *this is where I came in.*

'I said I'd try to help you,' he said slowly. 'But it's not like I have a program all set for activation. We're going to have to see how this plays out. You'd better be careful.'

Caitlin looked a little disappointed that he didn't have a quick fix, but finally she nodded. 'I'm just glad that there's somebody I can talk to about all this.' Her voice grew sharp.

'And you'd better be careful, too. I haven't heard from Rob since he sent me into your system. I've got no idea what he intends to do about you.'

'That's a nice thought,' Matt muttered. Then he said, 'Go on home. If I come up with anything, I'll talk to you tomorrow.'

Smiling gratefully, Cat Corrigan headed back to her car.

Matt waved, but he wasn't smiling as he watched the classic sportscar recede into the distance. If Cat had talked about Rob Falk earlier, maybe Gerald Savage would be alive now.

Somberly, Matt walked back to his house. His mother smiled when he came in. 'Is that the reason you decided not to go to your meeting? She seems like a nice girl. I don't think I've met her before.'

Matt could feel his face turning red. He wanted to say, 'She's a senator's daughter in a lot of trouble and she's only using me because she thinks I might be able to help her.'

Instead he shrugged and said, 'She's just a girl from school.'

His mom nodded. 'Yeah. And I can remember when your father was just a boy from school.'

Matt had nothing to say to that, so he just retreated to his room. He sat in his computer-link chair, but he still didn't want to enter his veeyar.

I've finally unmasked the Genius, he thought, *but I'm afraid to go after him with my computer.*

If he tried to go online and find out more about Rob Falk, it might warn the boy that Matt was on to him. But there was *something* he should be remembering . . .

Matt finally snapped his fingers. He had a bunch of stuff

downloaded from school last year, just compressed and left in memory until he sorted through or erased it.

Maybe now it's time to start sorting, Matt thought.

He ordered the computer to set up a holo-screen and began bursting out documents. Here was the school's virtual yearbook. Even though Rob Falk had left before the end of the year, his face was in the class pictures – they were shot early in the year. Matt silently shook his head as he zoomed in. Rob had obviously forgotten about picture day. He seemed to be a worse mess than Matt even remembered. His hair was all over the place, there was a stain on the collar of his shirt.

Matt banished the image. It made Rob look like a clown, when he knew the guy was a cold-blooded murderer. He turned to another file. Here was the school newspaper. Sometimes Matt ran through it, but even if he didn't, his school terminal was ordered to download, compress, and store, the *Bradford Bulletin*.

Wait a minute! That was why Matt remembered Rob Falk's name. Something in the paper . . .

Matt ordered his computer to burst out the newspaper files and scan them for Rob's name. It took several long minutes, but the computer was still faster than Matt would have been.

An image formed on the holo-screen. It was a story about a memorial service for Marian Falk, Rob's mother. She'd been crossing the street and become the victim of a hit-and-run.

Matt had often read about people's blood running cold. But this was the first time he'd actually felt it. Police had caught up with the driver, who'd turned out to be a middle-European diplomat, driving drunk. The man hadn't been brought up on charges, however, because he'd claimed diplomatic immunity. He'd run back to his home country, escaping scot-free.

That's right, Matt remembered. Rob Falk's father had been with the government, in the Customs Service. Ironically, his job had been to work with foreign diplomats about trade shipments entering and leaving the country.

There were no more references to Rob Falk in the newspaper, and Matt knew why. Mr Falk had not done well in his job after the accident. Things must not have been too pleasant at home, either. Rob's classwork began to suffer. David Gray had known the guy, and said that Rob had begun to lose himself in his computer. In the end, Mr Falk had lost his job and Rob had lost his Bradford scholarship.

Matt turned off his computer. A kid who'd retreated into his computer, who had good reasons to hate diplomats. Now he'd come back out, recruited a bunch of diplo-brats to commit illegal acts . . . and maybe had run one of them down, just as his mother had been run down.

From the moment Matt had promised to help Cat Corrigan, he'd known there was only one way out. He'd have to catch her alone tomorrow and somehow convince her to go to Net Force with the whole story. Maybe she and her friends could get off lightly, and Rob Falk might get some help.

The next day at school, Matt caught up with David Gray before they went in for Prep Period. 'You hear anything about Rob Falk anymore?' he asked.

David looked at him, his eyebrows rising. 'There's a name

I haven't heard in a while. No, I haven't heard from him since he crashed and burned.'

Matt winced, and David looked embarrassed. 'Guess that's not the best way to put it, considering what happened to his mom and all.'

'Do you think any of your friends might still be in touch with him?' Matt asked.

David shrugged. 'Let's go and find out.'

Matt knew a bit about computers, but David was really serious. And some of his pals could only be described as ultra-nerds. He led the way to a knot of sloppily dressed guys, who seemed to be arguing in another language. No, it was something about computer logic, but Matt was lucky if he understood one word in five.

'Anybody been hearing from Rob Falk?' David asked.

The nerds stared at him as if he'd just beamed in from another planet.

'Falk,' David went on. 'Used to go here last year. I think he was in the programming club.'

'Right, right,' one of the future scientists said. His hair was a wild mass of carrot-colored curls. 'Couldn't keep up anymore. Had to leave.'

'Family emergency,' a plump guy said.

Carrot Top gave him a lofty, 'as if that would mean anything' look. Then he pulled himself back to the real – boring – world. 'I haven't heard from him, neither voice nor e-mail.'

David looked around at the others, who shrugged.

'I'm afraid he wasn't really . . . tight . . . with anyone,' the plump boy said.

'He liked to work off on his own,' Carrot Top said.

Matt didn't dare look at David. Hearing that line from a group who looked like charter members of Dangerous Loners in Training, he was afraid he'd start to laugh.

The rest of the day wasn't funny, though. Once again, Matt had no chance of getting next to Cat Corrigan. In fact, he saw her only once in the halls, and that was at a distance.

As Matt headed for the lunchroom, he saw Sandy Braxton hurrying up and waving.

What is it with this guy? Matt wondered irritably. Is he that afraid of failing history?

'Hey, Matt! You've got a library period after this, right?'

Matt nodded.

'Great! I've got a datascrip of the Pickett's Charge re-enactment. They actually show Armistead getting hit and what happens afterwards.

'Great,' Matt echoed. Just at that moment, Cat Corrigan passed by, surrounded by what looked like an impenetrable wall of girl friends.

Matt was going to ask Sandy to sit with them, hoping to slip a note to Cat, but he was already moving off. 'I'm going to stop by the faculty room to get a research okay from Dr Fairlie. Meet you at the library.'

With a defeated shrug, Matt went in to find something to eat.

Walking down the hallway after lunch, Matt had no idea what he'd just eaten. He'd thought it was soybean mockmeat, but it seemed to leave a fish-oil aftertaste in his mouth.

I really should try and remember what it is, he told himself, *just so I can never order it again.*

He arrived in the library, where Sandy Braxton sat eagerly awaiting him. Mr Petracca, the librarian, took attendance, then Sandy went up and spoke quietly.

The librarian turned to his console, cued the holo-screen, and gave a couple of commands. 'Yes, the request from Dr Fairlie is in the system,' he said. Reaching under the desk, he pulled out a datascrip with a large number six on its label. 'You can use lab six,' Mr Petracca said.

Sandy marched out into the hall with a surprised Matt following. He'd expected to watch the re-enactment in holo, probably with a pair of earphones. Somehow, Sandy had wangled a visit to one of the veeyar labs!

'These re-enactment people must have plenty of bucks to create such a high-grade sim,' Matt said.

'Nothing but the best for the Virginia Volunteers,' Sandy assured him with a grin. 'This will be great! We'll be right in the center of the action!'

The veeyar labs were actually part of the library, overseen by Mr Petracca's console. They represented a serious invest-ment, even for a ritzy school like Bradford. Automated doors hissed open as the boys approached lab six. This was one of the smaller setups, with only four computer-link chairs. Matt realized with a slight shock that he'd recently been on the other side of the computer-link in this system. He and Caitlin had passed through the virtual chem lab on their way to Sean McArdle's press conference.

A small but extremely expensive computer console faced the four chairs. Sandy slipped in the school's datascrip, booting the computer for independent use. Then he reached into his pocket and came out with another datascrip. This one was decorated with the old Confederate flag, the stars and bars.

'What do you expect from an outfit called the Virginia Volunteers?' Sandy said with a grin. 'Of course they play a rebel unit!'

'You're not going to play the whole fight, are you Sandy?' Matt asked as the other boy went to insert the datascrip with the simulation. 'The artillery barrage went on for two hours.'

Sandy shook his head. 'Nah. We don't have time for that. I've got it cued from where the Confederates fire their rifles and make the final charge.' He gestured to the computer-link chairs. 'Plant it – we're almost ready.'

Matt took a seat, and so did Sandy. 'Computer, load Gettysburg simulation, from cue two-two-seven.'

Leaning back in the chair, Matt let the receptors tune into his implants. There was a slight feeling of disorientation, but it wasn't as noticeable as the brain-buzz that took place with his unit at home.

That's the mark of a really expensive system, he thought. He'd heard the best systems have no sensory threshold at all. You're just there in the sim.

He closed his eyes and found himself on a grassy hillside, a perfect place for a picnic – if the artillery barrage hadn't passed through. Trees had branches torn away. Some trunks had been shattered. A line of old-fashioned cannon stood in front of a stone wall. Some of the guns had been struck by incoming shells as well. The heavy metal tubes of some cannon barrels had been torn from their wooden carriages.

Matt gulped slightly when he saw the still, bloody forms of the cannoneers lying beside their wrecked guns.

Man, he thought, *they go all-out on these re-enactments*.

There was only one thing wrong with the picture. It was still a *picture*, incredibly realistic, but nothing was moving. The infantry crouching behind the stone wall were motionless. The blue-clad soldiers didn't even seem to breathe. The grass was absolutely still, not waving in the breeze.

'Whenever you're ready,' Sandy Braxton's voice called.

Matt turned, and his stomach did a flip-flop.

A long, ragged line of men in gray and brownish uniforms was coming up the hill, frozen in midstep. Information that he'd read came swimming up from his memory. The battle line had been a mile long, composed of fifteen thousand men. There were a lot fewer of them now, after marching almost half a mile through a storm of death. They looked grim, slightly hunched over as if they were walking into a stiff wind. Most of the men were bringing up their rifles to aim.

'Now I know how the little duck in the shooting gallery feels,' Matt joked. 'I really think we'd be better off watching this from behind the Confederate line.' He gestured toward the thousands of rifles. 'Looks like it's going to get a little noisy around here.'

'Suit yourself,' Sandy said, stepping through a gap in the line. 'Armistead ought to be over here, leading the left wing.'

When they reached what looked like a good vantage point, Sandy clapped his hands over his ears. 'Execute!' he yelled.

Matt quickly followed his example as the Confederate line suddenly leapt into life, aiming their weapons and firing.

The sound of the rifle fire wasn't what Matt had

expected. Instead of the sharp, metallic rap he was familiar with from the holos, these weapons gave off a base *fwoomp!* Accompanied by clouds of grayish powder-smoke.

The objectives ahead disappeared in the weapon-made haze, but the troops marched on.

'Watch carefully now,' Sandy advised. 'This next part is going to hurt.'

Even as he spoke, one of the soldiers in the line ahead suddenly whirled around and swung his musket. The rifle butt caught Sandy in the side of the head. He went down like a pole-axed steer.

Injured in veeyar!

Matt rushed to his classmate. But even as he moved, he saw that three soldiers were moving out of line to come toward him. Each of them had a bayonet on the end of his rifle barrel.

Taking a step back from Sandy, Matt watched the gleaming, foot-long lengths of steel swing to follow him.

He didn't know how the Genius – Rob Falk – had managed it.

But this sim had just changed from the Battle of Gettysburg to the fight of Matt's life!

Chapter 15

Matt backed away from the unconscious Sandy Braxton, his eyes on the three Confederate soldiers who'd left their places in the battle line. All around him, Pickett's Charge moved on to its bloody climax. But Matt had eyes only for the three socket bayonets aimed at him.

Maybe he should have been watching where he was going. His heel caught in something, and suddenly he was tumbling. He'd tripped over a dead or wounded attacker! Long-drilled training from the Net Force Explorers' dojo took over. Matt twisted even as he went down, lashing out with his hands to break his fall. He rolled as he hit the ground, quickly getting to his feet.

As he moved, his hand touched wood and metal. The wounded man's rifle!

Matt grabbed up the weapon as his three deadly enemies came running up. The one in the lead had a bushy brown beard and sergeant's stripes. The man behind him had a ferocious-looking black beard. The third was scarcely older than Matt, with just a couple of patches of hair on his chin.

The sergeant didn't wait for the other two, but launched an awkward attack on his own. Matt began to feel some hope. He wasn't facing trained soldiers, just interlopers who'd invaded this simulation. They didn't know how to handle their rifles.

Not that Matt was an expert. But he had worked out with pugil sticks – padded quarterstaffs – under the Net Force's Quantico-trained drill instructors. Those guys had been tough as Marines, and they'd at least thumped the basics of stick-fighting into the Net Force Explorers.

Matt parried the sergeant's wild thrust on the barrel of his borrowed rifle. He forced the bayonet down and aside. It stabbed uselessly past his left hip. Then Matt shifted his grip on the weapon, ramming the stock into his attacker's gut. The sergeant doubled over, and Matt smacked him in the head. The man was down before the other two had reached him.

'Computer!' Matt shouted. 'End simulation! Execute!'

Nothing happened. He was still trapped in the Gettysburg re-enactment, with a pair of guys who clearly meant no good, advancing on him with their bayonets at ready. His new attackers came on more cautiously after seeing what had happened to their pal.

Blackbeard went to the right while the Kid moved left, forcing Matt to divide his attention between them. He began backing up again, trying to keep some distance between them. 'Computer! Pause!' he yelled.

But the action kept unrolling around him. Whatever Rob Falk had done, he'd taken control of this system right out of Matt's hands.

The black-bearded soldier began a series of short jabs. Matt blocked them, then spun back and to his right, foiling an attempt by the other guy to get round behind him.

Matt brought up his rifle as if he were going to fire, sending both attackers scrambling back away from him. But as he tried to engage the weapon, the hammer fell with a dry *click*. Either the gun had already been fired, or it needed something that Matt didn't know about.

Blackbeard suddenly broke into a run, swinging his rifle in a wide, looping movement to slash with his bayonet. Matt braced himself to receive the attack. But suddenly, the black-bearded man was falling!

The look on his attacker's face would have been comical in any other situation. A brilliant red stain appeared on his gray uniform jacket, and down he went.

Matt couldn't help glancing at the Union battle line where jets of flame lanced from the muzzles of massed rifles. Did they have to worry about stray bullets on the battlefield?

No, that was impossible. This was a re-enactment, not the actual battle. They couldn't have been using live ammunition.

Then Matt realized. When Rob had sent his pals into the sim, he'd simply picked the three closest soldiers to Sandy and Matt. Now it turned out that one of those soldiers had been slated to become a casualty. His number had come up, and down he'd gone!

That meant Matt had only a lone opponent to face – for the moment. The youthful face opposite him looked a little worried as the Kid feinted and jabbed with his weapon.

Matt parried almost mechanically, his mind busy on something else. The 'death' of Blackbeard meant that Falk didn't have complete control over the simulation. The computer was still doing what it was programmed to do.

The Kid glanced over Matt's shoulder. That was the only warning he received. Matt thumped his opponent in the chest, knocking him back, and spun round as a Confederate officer lashed out with his sword. The blade made a chilling noise, worse than fingernails on a blackboard, as it scraped along Matt's rifle barrel. If he'd been a little slower, people would have had to call him Lefty!

Even if Falk didn't absolutely control the computer, he could keep sending his people back into the simulation. Just two of them, it seemed – maybe Matt had managed to hurt the third.

That didn't matter. Sooner or later, one of these clowns would score with a lucky shot.

And then Matt would suffer the fate of Gerry Savage.

Unless . . .

Matt retreated again as his attackers came in from opposite sides.

What was the first command Sandy had given the computer? The one that had set up this particular run of the simulation?

Hoping he'd gotten the numbers right, Matt shouted, 'Computer, reload Gettysburg simulation, cue two-two-seven!'

It was like time travel. Matt and Sandy were between the two battle lines. Nothing was moving – and that included Sandy. He lay on the weirdly stiff grass.

But Matt couldn't worry about that right now. His end run had succeeded! He'd managed to yank control of the computer back from Rob Falk!

'Computer!' he shouted quickly. 'Cancel. And exit!'

The slopes of Cemetery Hill winked out, and Matt was

back in veeyar lab six. He leapt from his computer-link chair. Sandy Braxton lolled in his seat, unconscious.

'Mister Braxton?' a voice suddenly filled the room. Matt recognized it as Mr Petracca, the school librarian. 'What's going on in there? My monitors are giving some very odd readings for that simulation you're running.'

'Something's gone wrong,' Matt called. 'Sandy Braxton is unconscious. I think the sim has been tampered with. Get the school doctor!'

Matt sat in the school office. Sandy was in the school's medical facility. Mr Petracca, the doctor, and a nurse had come bursting into veeyar lab six. Sandy was in shock, waiting for an Emergency Services ambulance. Matt was waiting for the police to arrive so he could give a statement.

Like it or not, it looked as if he'd have to blow the lid off Rob Falk and the virtual vandals before he spoke to Cat Corrigan.

At that moment, Caitlin walked into the office.

The two of them stared at one another. Then, at almost the same time, they asked, 'What are *you* doing here?'

Cat responded first. 'I was pulled out of class. There was a message from my father's office. He's sick – he collapsed. I'm just checking in before I go home.'

She looked at him, expecting his answer.

'Finish what you've got to do, first,' Matt muttered.

Caitlin got a pass from the office staff, and Matt walked her to the door. 'Sandy Braxton picked up a sim for the research project we're working on,' Matt said quietly when they were in the hall. 'We were in the veeyar lab, when things began to go very, very wrong.'

She stared at him. 'How wrong?'

'It was the re-creation of a famous battle. But some of the soldiers departed from their programming and began attacking us.'

Cat's eyes went wide. 'Oh, no!'

She turned back to the office. 'Where's Sandy?'

'He's going to the hospital. As far as I can tell, he's no worse off than the people who got shot at Camden Yards.' Matt's voice was grim. 'I don't know how *I'd* have ended up, though, with three guys with bayonets coming after me.'

Whatever color was left in Caitlin's face just drained away. 'Rob!' she whispered fiercely. 'It has to be Rob!' She looked sick. 'One of the first places we stuck trapdoors was in the school's veeyar system. I never thought—'

'Neither did I,' Matt admitted. 'I should have been more careful, especially since we passed through one of the veeyar system sites on our way to see Sean McArdle.'

Still, Caitlin looked as if she blamed herself for the ordeal Sandy and Matt had gone through.

Matt took her arm. 'Where's your car?'

'In the lot out back,' Caitlin said. 'I was kinda late getting in today.'

'I'll walk you out.' Matt's brain was going into overdrive. The cops would be arriving any minute. It was now or never to convince Cat to cooperate with the police and Net Force.

'This has gotten way out of control,' he told Caitlin as they stepped out of the rear exit of the school. 'You know already that you can't control Rob Falk. Isn't it time to admit you can't keep protecting him, either?'

'It's not like I have a choice!' Cat cried. 'Rob is—'

'Rob'll be mad at you, if you keep flappin' your mouth about him,' a voice interrupted.

Matt turned from Caitlin in complete shock. He hadn't expected to find anyone in the school parking lot during classes.

Instead, there were three kids surrounding the doorway. And no way were they Bradford students. They wore ripped jeans and armless shirts over T-shirts, bandannas, gold jewelery. One was a big, husky kid with dirty blond hair – the accent of the mountains was still thick in his voice. To his right was a wiry Asian youth, while the boy on the left seemed to mix several nationalities and races.

Though these street kids all looked wildly different, Matt noticed that each of them was wearing some combination of green and black.

Gang members.

Matt couldn't believe that they were being confronted by gangbangers at the doors of Bradford Academy. But there was no arguing with the evidence of his own eyes.

And there was no arguing with the gun the blond kid suddenly whipped from behind his baggy shirt. 'Let's have the car keys, honey.'

They were marched across the pavement to Caitlin's car. It was lucky she hadn't taken the Copperhead today. Even so, it was a tight squeeze for the five of them. The blond boy sat in front behind the steering wheel with Cat beside him. Matt was in the back seat, wedged between the other two.

'Tuck your hands under your butt,' the blond boy had ordered as Matt sat down. 'I don't want to see you moving a muscle. 'Cause if you do, Ng here will have to use this.' He handed the pistol to the Asian boy. 'And what he'll do is blow a big ol' hole through the front seat and right into this pretty li'l girl here.'

The big guy nodded at Caitlin, who sat frozen in the passenger's seat.

'Wh-where are you taking us?' she asked in a strangled voice.

'Why, we're takin' you to see Rob Falk,' the big blond boy said as he twisted the key in the ignition and started the engine.

'Seems only fair, with you takin' such an interest in him an' all.'

Chapter 16

Sitting on his hands in the back seat of Caitlin's car, Matt could only watch helplessly as the blond boy pulled out of the Bradford Academy parking lot.

If I were alone, I might just make a try for old Ng over there, Matt thought, looking at the wiry Asian boy with the pistol. Net Force instructors were Marine-trained, and expected everyone connected with the agency – even the young Explorers – to have some self-defense ability. Matt had done fairly well in his unarmed combat courses. If he only had himself to worry about, he might have been able to get the gun from Ng's hand.

But he couldn't be sure of getting the gun before one shot went off. And the way things were set up, that shot would go into Cat Corrigan's back.

So Matt sat where he was, grimly trying to memorize the route they were taking.

They quietly wove their way through local streets until they reached the Rock Creek Parkway. The blond boy pulled onto a northbound entrance ramp.

Sure, Matt thought. *The Beltway.*

Many years before, city planners had completely ringed

the District of Columbia with highways, so that drivers could avoid the traffic of the city's center. Improved transportation had also started a boom in the Maryland and Virginia suburbs. Housing developments were laid out, malls, office complexes – by the 1980s, sharp Washington business and government types were known as 'Beltway Bandits.'

But even by the turn of the century, things were changing. As improvements were made in the city, problems emerged in the inner suburbs – those inside the ring of roads. Ironically, they were the sort of 'city problems' that people had moved to suburbia to ignore. Immigrants. Poverty. Drugs. Gangs.

Cities, in spite of their problems, have business districts and lots of people to act as a tax base. The suburban towns found their police and social services overwhelmed.

Wherever they were going, Matt was sure it would be somewhere inside the Beltway.

The boy behind the wheel upped the speed, moving along with the flow of highway traffic.

'Nice,' said the boy at Matt's left. 'Is a nice car, Willy, no?'

'Nice car, yes,' Willy, the blond boy, said from behind the wheel. 'Light-years past my daddy's pickup. Too bad we have to dump it.'

On Matt's right, Ng jumped in surprise. 'We don't keep?'

Willy jerked his head at Caitlin. 'This little girl is a senator's daughter. Word gets out she's been snatched, we're gonna have the FBI and all the rest of the alphabet after us. Army, Navy, Marines, Coast Guard, who knows what-all?'

The other boy made a disappointed sound.

'No way, Mustafa. We don't want to be anywhere near this car when the gov-boys find it. So we leave it where other folks will find it first. Leave them to get the blame.'

Willy exited the Beltway and drove along an access road to a seedy-looking mall. The place had probably been built before the turn of the century, and whatever shine the buildings might have had once was long gone. Half the store fronts were empty, and some of those had holes in the windows. The other places were what Matt's father would call 'junk stores,' full of cheap, shoddy merchandise with big signs about bargains in the windows.

Matt noticed a phony-looking electronics store with a banner screaming about the tremendous buys inside. The glaring colors had faded in the sunshine, and there were tears in the plastic.

This is exactly the kind of place where you could buy a cheap antique of a computer, he suddenly thought. *Except they'd probably try to hold you up for too high a price.*

They thudded their way across the cracked concrete parking lot until Willy brought them to a halt next to a beat-up sedan.

It was hard to tell what color the car had been originally. One door was bluish-gray, and a fender was green. The rest seemed to be beige, except for the leprous gray spots of body putty.

'Everybody out,' Willy ordered.

Willy hopped from behind the wheel and got a firm hold on Caitlin's arm. In his other hand he had a Bowie knife, which he quickly showed to Matt, then lowered the weapon to the side of his leg where it wasn't so obvious to the people passing by on the street. 'Just so you don't try anything stupid-like,' the boy said, in his back-country drawl.

Ng held his gun down against his leg, but Matt knew he could have it up and shooting in a moment. Part of him was amazed that these guys were so cool about showing weapons so openly. But then again, they weren't doing anything to catch anyone's attention. They were just transferring themselves from a late-model car to a beat-up old rattletrap.

The seating arrangements were just the same. Matt was in the back, sandwiched between Ng and Mustafa, sitting on his hands. He wondered if they were going to fall asleep there under his butt.

Willy sat behind the wheel, his knife having disappeared as miraculously as it had leapt into his hand. Caitlin had the passenger's seat, right in front of Ng's gun.

People still called that the death seat, Matt suddenly remembered. He tried to push the thought out of his head.

Willy started the engine, and the clunker lurched forward ahead of a cloud of bluish smoke. 'You be careful with that gun, you hear?' he ordered Ng. 'I don't want you makin' no useless holes in this here seat. When we finish, this car's gonna be mine.'

Matt twisted to look out the filthy rear windshield at Cat's car.

'Left the keys on the front seat,' Willy said. 'Somebody'll be moving it along any minute now.'

They headed back to the Beltway and began retracing their path – probably to throw off anyone who might have been tracing Caitlin's car, Matt realized.

Their counterclockwise journey took them across the

Potomac River above the northwest section of D.C., halfway around the city, then across the much wider expanse of the river south of the city on the Woodrow Wilson Bridge.

They left the Beltway on the first exit past the bridge, entering southwest Washington. This was still a decayed neighborhood. Willy pulled into a no-game gas station and drove right into the mechanic's bay. A man was running a rag over a delivery van. When he saw the newcomers, he just walked away.

'Change your partners, once again,' Willy said. 'You'll get to sit in the back with your pal,' he told Caitlin. 'And with my pals, too,' he added.

The back of the van was a little roomier, Matt had to admit. He and Caitlin sat side by side. Ng and Mustafa sat across from them. The Asian boy still covered them with Willy's pistol.

Matt's main complaint was that he couldn't see where they were going. The rear of the van was completely enclosed. They were in a dark box, heading who knew where. Judging by the speed they were traveling, Matt figured that Willy was back on a parkway.

But then they got off, went through several turns, and came to a stop. Willy opened the rear door. Matt noticed he had his knife in his hand again. 'We're here,' the blond boy announced. 'Shake a leg, you two.'

Willy pulled Caitlin out, keeping his grip on her wrist. Then it was Matt's turn. He was very conscious of Ng with the gun behind him. Matt tried to take in his surroundings, but all he got was a quick glimpse of red brick before Willy gave him a not-too-gentle smack in the head with the hilt of his knife.

'You ain't here to play tourist. Just watch where you're walkin'. Let's go.'

They were hustled to a scarred wooden door which swung open just as they reached it. Inside was a reception committee – another trio of tough-looking street kids, each carrying a military rifle.

Matt paused in the doorway, his nose wrinkling at the mixed smells of sweat, beer, mildew, and rotting wood. Mustafa shoved him through.

'Went like a piece of cake,' Willy said. 'We picked her up with no problem, and this one was with her.' He nodded at Matt. 'Lucky thing Rob showed us pictures of all the suckers.'

He made his knife disappear, but kept his grip on Caitlin's arm. 'Come on along,' Willy said. 'We got some people want to see you.'

The prisoners were marched into what had probably been a cozy parlor about a hundred and twenty years ago. Now it was just a ruin. A couple of strips of wallpaper still dangled on the walls, but they were mainly defaced plaster. A couple of big pieces of furniture that no one had bothered to take with them sat rotting against the walls. They'd been moved to clear a space in the middle of the room, where a couple of tables held maps, papers, and a collection of mismated, old-fashioned computers.

Two figures stood in the improvised command center – Matt recognized the setup immediately. Then he realized that one of the gang members looked familiar.

Rob Falk was a little taller than the mental image Matt had kept of him. His skinny frame had put on some muscle. His chest was thicker, and Matt could see the sinews in the bare arms he showed in his sleeveless gang shirt.

'A little different from the gawky wimp at Bradford, huh?' Falk gave Matt and Caitlin a sort of sneering smile. 'That's what happens when you get stuck on the wrong side of the Beltway. For a while there, it was touch and go. Then I met James—'

'No last names,' growled the big black guy standing next to Rob. He was built like a wrestler, with arms as big as most people's legs, a shaved head, and grim, almost glaring, black eyes.

'James is the warlord of the Buzzards, one of the many . . . ah, voluntary organizations available for suburban youth.' Rob's lips quirked. 'Yeah, I know, the new technological opportunities combined with urban renewal were supposed to mean the end of the old street gangs. It didn't happen. When the people who got displaced from their old neighborhoods arrived in the suburbs, they found a stew just simmering. All kinds of immigrants, legal and illegal. Salvadorans, Mexicanos, Cubans, Nigerians, Jordanians, Pakistanis, refugees from the Balkans. Plus, there were people just coming to the big city. You met Willy? His parents grew up in a coal-mining town in Appalachia – until the coal ran out. Lots of folks have come to this country – this city – in search of a better life.'

He laughed. 'I sound like a damn politician, don't I?' Then the laughter left his voice. 'Instead, they were stuck out along the Beltway. None of these folks have found a place in your brave new world . . . but they did find a place in the Buzzards – a fine gang with a tradition that goes back a good seventy-five years, now.'

'And the Buzzards found you,' Matt added.

Rob gave him the same look that Dr Fairlie used for a good answer. 'Very good!'

He nodded to the big guy beside him. 'James saw that I understood the new technology and could use it. We had a rough time at first, scraping the necessary hardware together. Finally, we ended up heisting a couple of these so-called appliance stores.'

'Got a couple of good holo-sets out of the deal, too,' Willy said.

'It's mostly junk, of course, especially compared to the systems you're used to,' Rob went on. 'But I managed. Compiled some pretty good programs, didn't I?' His smile became shark-like. 'Good enough to sucker in the great Cat Corrigan and her friends from many lands.'

He shook his head at Matt, making a 'naughty-naughty' gesture with his finger. 'I can't figure out how you got involved in all this, Hunter. From what I remember, you always seemed a pretty level-headed, safe and sane, *boring* guy. But then,' Rob looked over at Caitlin. 'I guess you wouldn't be the first to be led astray by a pretty face.'

'Why did you drag us here?' Cat demanded.

'You looked about ready to blab,' Rob said, 'And we don't want you blabbing about what we've been up to.'

'Was that why you killed Gerry?'

Matt gave Caitlin a glance from the corner of his eye. As helpless prisoners, now was not the time to start annoying Rob and his buddy James.

'Gerry was turning into a loose cannon,' the gang warlord said flatly. 'That stunt he pulled with the Irish could have caught the wrong people's attention.'

'I thought you'd be more upset about our attempt to kill

your new friend over here,' Rob said with a nod for Matt. 'That was pretty clever how you got out of there, Hunter. Of course, I was working third-hand from this pile of—' He paused for a moment. 'If I had a first-rate system, they'd still be spooning your brains off the comp-link in veeyar lab six!'

Matt shrugged. 'Yeah, well, I guess we all have our disappointments. Frankly, I think you went a little overboard. I couldn't figure out what you were doing. And from the way they were acting, Caitlin and the others didn't have a clue, either.'

'Maybe not,' Rob said. 'But they might give a clue to other people, if they gave up a full list of the systems they'd visited.'

He sighed. 'I really thought they'd hunker down and keep their mouths shut until we were completely ready. You know how those people love their reputations. But then you came along and started rocking the boat. Savage began acting crazy, and the others became . . . unreliable. We've had to push up our timetable, and shut some mouths.'

'Your timetable?' Matt tried to get a look at the map taped to the tabletop. It was upside-down from his point of view, but he could see it was a point of land jutting out into the joining point of two rivers. Somehow, it looked familiar, but Matt couldn't place it.

'You've got to forgive me but I still have no idea what you're talking about,' Matt said. 'What were the virtual vandals doing for you, besides causing confusion?'

Rob Falk gave him that shark's smile again. 'If they confused you, then they did their job perfectly. Cat and her not-so-diplomatic friends were supposed to raise a fair amount of hell to keep the law's attention on them.'

He paused, and thumped his fist down on the map. 'While all the time, they were opening a way for us to get into the Gardens at Carrollsburg.'

Chapter 17

'*WHAT?*'

Matt knew his voice was too loud, but he couldn't help it. At last he recognized the map on the Buzzards' command post table.

He'd seen it on his computer only a few days ago. It showed the layout of the Gardens at Carrollsburg, the gated community Sandy Braxton's father was making so much money from.

But what could Rob – and his fellow gangbangers – possibly want with anything there?

He wondered as much out loud.

James and Rob laughed.

'I'll show you,' the gang's computer whiz said. He stepped round to his patched-together computer and began inputting orders – on a keyboard! Matt hadn't even seen one of those outside of a museum.

How old is that thing? Matt wondered.

Old or not, however, it worked. A grainy, fuzzy hologram swam into view over the computer system.

Matt recognized it as a briefing map, the sort of visual aid shown to troops about to go on maneuvers – or on a real attack. It was a larger version of the map on the table, showing the point of land at the junction of the Potomac and Anacostia Rivers. Instead of showing streets, however, this map was broken into large, vividly colored areas. The tip and eastern side of the peninsula was colored blue with a red and white border. 'That's Fort McNair – an army base,' Rob explained. 'From there up the Potomac to the Tidal Basin, there are expensive condominiums.'

Then he pointed at a green area covering most of the remaining land in the peninsula. 'The Gardens at Carrollsburg – a regular garden spot now. Gated community, rush-hour hovercraft service up the Potomac, just lovely. Named after the town of Carrollsburg which stood on this land before the city of Washington was even thought of.'

Falk grinned at the prisoners, the light reflecting from the holo turning his face into a devil's mask. 'But in between the colonial town and this outpost of gracious living, the area had another name.'

Matt remembered just as Rob spoke.

'Buzzard Point.'

Rob gave Matt a surprised look. 'Very good,' he complimented. 'And you said you weren't coming up with anything.'

'One of the Leets in school – his father invested in the development. The name came up again when I was trying to track down kids who might have been involved with your vandals. Their addresses seemed to cluster in certain zip codes – Georgetown or the northwest, or 20024 in the southwest. That seems to be where the diplomats are found . . .'

Matt's voice trailed off as he realized that these were the people Rob had a special reason to hate. They'd cost him his mother, his father's job, his school, his whole life.

But Falk didn't fly off the handle. He simply nodded. 'Before all those – nice people – moved in, this area was home turf for the Buzzards. Get it now? The gang took its name from the neighborhood.'

'Not the prettiest handle,' James growled, glancing around at the ruined walls surrounding them. 'But then, it wasn't the prettiest neighborhood, either.'

Rob turned back to the holo-map glowing in midair. 'Go a little farther north, and it still isn't.' He pointed to a large, bright orange blob across the top of the peninsula. 'This whole area is still waiting to be renovated. Part of it will be an expansion of the Gardens at Carrollsburg, but other developers are getting into the act, too. The people who lived here were moved out, but the bulldozers haven't come in yet.'

He ran his finger around the irregular orange borders. 'All this space between those rich, fat diplomats and the gentrified neighborhoods coming down from the Mall and Capitol Hill.' Then his hand punched through the orange empty area. 'Sort of like a no-man's-land, cutting off the whole Carrollsburg gated community.'

His voice sounded faraway, thoughtful, but his face was tight. 'They think they're so safe behind their gates and their security. Ha! That stuff is as solid as Swiss cheese. Cat and her friends have riddled the place with trapdoor programs. I can get into dozens of home systems in there now. And those computers all tie in to the hardware that runs the whole development.'

There was an ugly, scary light in Rob Falk's eyes as he turned to Matt and Caitlin . . . and this time it didn't come from the garish colors of the holographic map he'd been pointing to.

'I've got dozens of doors to reach in and cut their communications, turn off their alarms, kill their power. I can lock those precious gates of theirs, stranding them inside.' His voice took on a gloating tone. 'Or I could open those gates up to let in a couple of hundred uninvited guests.'

Matt's eyes shot from Rob to his new friend James.

'We got Buzzards from all around the Beltway gathering here,' the gang warlord assured him. 'All of them will be carrying.'

'Carrying?' Caitlin said.

James gave her a scornful look. 'Guns, girl. What you think we'd be carrying?'

'They really don't have enough guards in the compound,' Rob said.

'Just enough to sit on their fat butts at the gates and direct traffic,' James agreed.

Rob laughed. 'But then, who'd expect an invasion in such a classy neighborhood?'

'It'll be the biggest rip-off in Washington history,' James boasted.

'At least since the British burnt down the White House in 1814.' An ugly look of triumph covered Rob's face. 'House after house full of diplomats – and not one of them will have any immunity.'

'You're crazy!' Cat Corrigan burst out.

Matt gave her another look. He might agree with her, but

he knew it wasn't healthy to point out facts like that to crazy people.

'Even if you pull off this "rip-off" you're talking about, you'll have more than the police after you. You'll have people whose reach doesn't end with the D.C. line. The State Department will have to get involved if you molest diplomats. And the rest of the Feds will be right behind them – the Attorney General, the FBI, Net Force, and who knows what other agencies?'

'You left out the Congress, rushing to rescue Senator Corrigan's little girl,' Rob Falk mocked.

'We got it figured out,' James assured them. 'In quick, slap those rent-a-cops down, grab what we can, then out even quicker. Before the big shots know anything happened, we'll be spread all over the Beltway. It's like a guerrilla war, baby. They won't know where to look to find whoever is responsible.'

Rob Falk leaned forward. 'But just in case, we'll provide the perfect high-profile fall guys for the media and politicians to blame.'

He poked contemptuous fingers at Caitlin and Matt. 'Think of the fun some people could have carrying on about a bunch of wild diplo-brats, a senator's daughter, and a military bureaucrat's wannabe son, all taking a walk on the wild side?'

Matt felt sick. He could just imagine the media circus. Their faces smeared over every holo-news program, in the broadcast magazines and the sleazy gossip-fests that pretended to be news shows. The preaching and the finger-pointing by self-appointed guardians of morality and political opportunists. Dad would be laughed out of class.

Mom would never get another promotion again. Cat's father would probably have to get out of politics. And the diplomats would have to go pack up and go home.

Unless . . .

'Maybe you've got us,' Matt bluffed, 'but I don't see Luc Valery or Serge Woronov. Do you think they're going to sit around quietly when they hear that Caitlin has been kidnapped? Especially since you killed Savage.'

Loud laughter drowned out his words. Rob Falk just waved his argument away. 'Already taken care of.'

Caitlin looked as sick as Matt felt. 'Y-you mean you k-k-killed—?'

James was already shouting through the doorway on the other side of the room. Seconds later, a couple more husky Buzzards gangbangers led in two bedraggled figures.

The warlord laughed as if he'd heard a great joke. 'We nabbed them *before* we took care of you.'

Luc Valery was dressed in an expensive suit – or what was left of an expensive suit. At the right shoulder of his jacket, the arm had almost been torn off. It hung crazily, held in place only by the pale silk inner lining. Serge wore jeans and a sweater – and a huge, swollen black eye.

Rob gave the diplo-brats the same kind of smile a cat would give lame canary. 'Luc was supposed to be going to lunch with his dad – until he heard this.'

He hit some keys on the keyboard, and suddenly the floating map was replaced by an image of Caitlin. 'I've got to talk with you – right away.' Her voice turned to a breathless whisper. 'That guy who's been pestering us – I think he's the one who drove that car that got Gerry!'

Rob turned to the speechless Caitlin. 'Pretty effective, don't you think? Of course, I've been sampling your voice for months, just in case I needed to imitate you. The gallant M'sieu Valery rushed to the meeting place your virtual version suggested – then wound up coming along here with just a little persuasion.'

He turned to the other foreign prisoner. 'Now Serge – he was a bit more of a challenge. Although he goes out to play on the Net pretty much as often as he likes, the security people from *Slobodan Narodny* try to keep an eye on their ambassador's son. So we needed to give him a strong reason to ditch any trailing bodyguards. Luckily, I had the perfect button to push.'

Rob turned to Matt. 'I borrowed your stick-man and put him together with the Idiom Savant program.'

Another set of keys pushed, and the hologram changed to Leif Anderson's whimsical stick-figure spitting words in Serbo-Croatian. Serge gave a roar and tried to pull free of the two guys holding onto him. In seconds, however, they had him efficiently – and brutally – pinned to the floor.

'In case you're wondering, that speech your proxy is sprouting runs something along the lines of "give me money or I spill everything to your father and his government." It's a little more insulting and nasty in the Balkan version.'

Shaking his head, Rob gave another chuckle. 'You should be glad old Serge never saw your face,' he told Matt. 'When he went to meet with you to pay the first instalment, he was carrying this—'

Rob reached into his back pocket and pulled out an old semi-automatic pistol. It was an ancient Army M9, the Beretta 9mm. sidearm used around the turn of the century.

Probably it had gone off to the Balkans with one of the many peacekeeping forces sent there over the years, been lost, used by several sides in the seemingly never-ending wars and feuds in the region, and now returned to the United States in somebody's diplomatic luggage.

'Luckily, our reception committee was able to take it away from him before anybody got hurt.'

Rob glanced at Serge, who lay groaning under the weight of his two guards. 'At least,' he amended, 'before anyone got hurt too badly.'

Luc Valery stared wildly down at his friend, at the guards, at the other prisoners, and finally at Rob. 'Who are you?' he demanded. 'What do you want?'

Rob gave him a slow, insolent grin. 'I'm your fairy godfather, Froggie-boy,' he said. 'Thanks to me, you got to go out and play to your heart's content on the Net, doing things nice kids would never be allowed to do. I gave you interesting shapes to use, doorways to come back and have fun, and, yeah, the occasional order. I'm Rob Falk.'

'You're a coward and a killer,' Luc accused. 'You murdered Gerald Savage – or, more likely, you ordered one of these thugs to do the job.'

'Actually,' Rob said, 'my friend James here volunteered to take care of it. But then, he never liked loud-mouthed bigots. Especially foreign loud-mouthed bigots.'

Luc turned bright red. The veins popped up on the side of his head and the cords in his neck stood out through the skin. 'You don't know what a mistake you've made! My father is a representative of the French government! He has the ear of the ambassador! And as you said, Serge's father *is* the ambassador for Slobodan Narodny! Whatever you're planning, you'll never get away with it! Our voices will be heard! And our governments will demand that you and your – associates – receive the proper punishment!'

Matt thought the young Frenchman was going to hurl himself across the table and take Rob Falk down. Certainly Rob's friend James expected it. He pulled a pistol, aiming it at Luc. The remaining guard grabbed the diplomat's son, too.

But Rob's face hadn't even changed expression. He'd listened to Luc's tirade as if the other boy were suggesting that it might rain that evening.

'I suppose that's true,' Rob said. 'You guys – except for Matt here – are all pretty important.'

'Depend on it!' Luc threatened. 'We'll tell—'

'*LET ME FINISH!*' The words rapped out as if they were being hammered on steel. For one second, the incandescent hatred that Rob Falk held for all diplomats blazed across his face and eyes. Then, as if he were slipping on a mask – or donning a proxy – he returned to the distant, ironic pose he'd used in talking to the prisoners.

'I suppose you might tell someone what went on here,' Rob said mildly, 'If you were still alive.' He raised the old pistol and aimed it carefully. 'Fortunately, that won't be an issue.'

Chapter 18

Rob Falk and his friend James, the warlord of the Buzzards, filled the sudden silence with loud, harsh laughter. Rob lowered his gun.

The young computer genius stuck the pistol in his back pocket. 'Oh, we're not gonna do it *now*,' he said, as if this should make the prisoners feel better. 'But we really have to shut your mouths. After all, you only served two uses for us. You could get into places that my friends and I – well, I guess you'd say we were a little too rough for polite society.'

James laughed again, but Rob went on. 'The other use was to take the heat – create big headlines and make the big-time commentators and politicians buzz and moan about the state of young people today.' He sneered. 'Why should we go to all the trouble of creating scapegoats if they're just going to point the finger at us?'

'You got a point there, brother,' James said.

'Besides, if you die, there'll be just enough tragedy to keep the publicity machine running overtime.' Rob might have been discussing how to talk up an upcoming dance, or how to get the word out about a charity car-wash. Matt had never heard something so *evil* discussed so casually.

'So that's it?' Cat said in a shocked voice. 'You've used us up, so now you throw us away?'

Rob turned, grinned, and nodded. 'Go to the head of the class! That's *exactly* it! Just like you and your so-important friends use people and toss them away. Of course, we have to make it a little more permanent. But then, we're playing for higher stakes than a good grade in Bonehead Computing.'

His voice dripped phony compassion as he leaned toward the girl. 'Oh, I know it's tough. All this time, you've grown up thinking you were a human being with rights and privileges. Well, I'm sorry, honey. But you've got to learn it's different out here in the cold, cruel world. My mom thought she was a human being. But some drunk, rich diplomat saw her as an obstacle – or maybe as a target.'

The false sympathy was gone from his voice. Each word came out as if it were chipped from ice. 'We'll never know what was going through his mind. He hightailed it back to Whatzislavia as soon as his ambassador pried him away from the police. Now, it's too bad you don't have an ambassador to go to bat for you. We don't need another pretty face around here. We don't need your daddy's money. We need someone to take the heat for us after this operation goes down. And you're elected. Grow up and face it, girl. It's the last thing you might do in this life.'

It was a cruel little speech, but Caitlin wouldn't give Rob the satisfaction of seeing tears. The effort made her shake, but she stood straight and glared at him.

'Good work!' Rob applauded. 'See, you're growing up already.'

He turned his attention to the other prisoners. 'Okay,

now, I expect you guys to be cool. Keep annoying us—' he looked especially at Serge as he spoke – 'and you'll wind up with marks that will make it harder for us to set the right picture. We want the public to see a bunch of rich, privileged kids who got in with the wrong crowd and came to a sorry end. Behave yourself, and I promise your sorry end will be relatively painless. Give us trouble, and we'll hurt you before this is over. Then we'll have to come up with a nasty end to hide what we did. You'll end up flipping a car and being burned to death. Or maybe even have your cruel gangbanger pals kill you execution-style.'

'And what happens if we're good boys and girls?' Matt asked, amazed that his voice stayed steady. 'What nice way will you use to kill us then?'

'Well, there is no nice way,' Rob admitted. 'Maybe we'll get you drunk or high so you'll scarcely feel somebody's home security system taking you out.'

He glanced around. 'So, if there are no more questions – and I really hope no more "you can't get away with this" comments – it's time to get to work!'

For one wild moment, Matt was tempted to reveal his Net Force connection and tell Falk that he was working undercover. That would have ripped away his condescending attitude.

Of course, it would also probably get Matt killed immediately.

No, he'd keep quiet, wait, and try to pull off the duty of every prisoner – to escape.

That, of course, would depend on wherever Rob and his gangbanger friends decided to store their captives.

Since no one had anything more to say, Rob and James

declared their little meeting over. The guards closed in around Matt, Caitlin, Luc, and Serge, and began herding them through the door in the far wall of the room – the door the boys had come through earlier.

They went out of the room, then down a short, dark hallway ending at a big, heavy oak door, the kind you couldn't buy anymore. Not that anybody would want this one, Matt thought. The heavy wood panel was torn and gouged. There were even a couple of bullet holes, as if someone had used it for target practice.

But the door was still able to block out sound. Matt was surprised at the noise level on the other side when the guards pushed the door open. He was even more surprised when he went through the doorway into a huge, high-ceilinged room filled with row after row of scarred wooden pews. They were in a church!

A quick glance told him that it had to be an abandoned church. Leaks from the steeply angled roof had caused huge smears down the dingy walls, rotting the plaster away from the red brick beneath. Most areas were thick with dust, except for the pews. They were thick with people, but these people hadn't come to pray.

The congregation consisted of hard young men, many younger than Matt, then ranging in age on up to a couple of guys who looked to be in their late twenties. Beefy or rail-thin, black-skinned, brown, or pale and freckled, they all had the same wary, street-smart hardness. And whatever they wore – most were in jeans and shirts with the sleeves torn away – their outfits mixed the colors green and black.

There had to be a couple of hundred of them, smoking, laughing, checking their guns. Yes, each young man was armed. Hunting rifles, stolen armory weapons, and every variety of pistol Matt had ever heard about seemed to be on display. There were even a couple of antique Beretta M9s like the one Rob Falk had waved around.

This was Rob's strike force, the fighting strength of the Buzzards called together at their warlord's orders.

They fell into a dangerous silence for a second as they saw strangers coming through the door. But James came in after them, and the warlord was definitely in a cheerful mood. 'Be nice to these people, now,' he warned his troops. 'They're the ones who're helping us to get into the Gardens at Carrollsburg!'

A roar filled the air like nothing that had been heard in that church before – half ironic cheer, half wolf's snarl at sighting red meat.

James gestured to Matt and Caitlin. 'Put these where you kept the others. And no foolin' around with 'em! We want them all in one piece for when we need them.'

Matt and the others were marched down the aisle to the rear of the church until Matt thought they were going out. But before they reached the church doors, the lead guard turned aside, to the gaping entrance of a dusty stairwell.

Are they sticking us in the choir loft? Matt wondered. But the stairs kept going up until Matt realized they were climbing inside the church's steeple. The next step was a moldy wooden ladder leaning drunkenly against the lip of a trapdoor overhead.

Matt climbed and found himself in a space a little larger than his bedroom – but a lot taller. Once bells had hung here, rung on feast days and to celebrate marriages. They were gone now, probably taken when the church was deconsecrated. A bell is a valuable thing, even if it's just melted down for its metal.

This space was empty, except for dust, the remains of a couple of bird nests, and what looked like mouse droppings on the floor. Four reasonably clean folding chairs were scattered around. Apparently, they'd been brought up for the comfort of the prisoners.

Caitlin, Luc, and Serge had all reached the upper story now. From below came a scraping sound. Their guards were removing the ladder!

'Y'all just sit quiet up there,' Willy's voice echoed up the steeple. 'We'll come fetch you when we're ready to move.'

As soon as the guards were out of sight, Matt snatched up one of the chairs and pushed it against the wall. The belfry had no windows, but above their heads, the enclosure was open to the air. This was where the sound of the bells had rung out in the old days.

In later years, there must have been a problem with intruders. Iron bars, spaced five inches apart, wouldn't have blocked the tolling of the bells. But they'd keep anyone out of the belfry – or in.

The bars didn't block the view, though, as Matt pulled himself up on his improvised stepstool. He looked out – upon a vista of empty, crumbling buildings. The roofs of the surrounding stone and wooden row houses seemed to sag as if the weight of too many years pressed down on them. Paint peeled off the siding boards like diseased, scabby skin, revealing the gray of moldering wood. Obviously, it hadn't been a great neighborhood even when people lived here. Scattered among the houses were square, raw brick buildings. They housed auto-body repair shops, chemical warehouses, all the parts of a city that get shoved into out-of-the-way corners where nice people didn't have to look at – or live – with them.

It did keep the rents down, of course. Poor folks were expected to put up with the noise and the corrosive smells. This was a neighborhood that had been hard-used. And once it was deserted, the buildings, both old and new, were quickly falling into ruin.

To Matt, it looked like a town abandoned in the face of an enemy army's advance. No-man's-land. But where would you find such a desolate area in the middle of a teeming cityscape like greater Washington?

No-man's-land! The words seemed to echo in Matt's thoughts as he scampered down from the chair and dragged it to another wall. Nearby, he saw a similar blasted landscape. But farther off, he saw apartment towers rising over the rooftops. And right in front of the church steeple ran an elevated expressway with cars zipping along. Rays of late-afternoon sunshine streamed between the bars. That way had to be west.

Matt dropped to the floor and hauled the chair so he was facing south. More devastated buildings, and a muddy scar where old houses had been bulldozed. Beyond that, however, rose a wall of rosy brick, enclosing expensive-looking brick and paneled buildings that looked like they'd escaped from Colonial Williamsburg. Expensive cars stood in driveways surrounded by brilliant green lawns.

Letting go of the bars, Matt dropped back to the belfry floor again.

'What did you see?' Caitlin demanded.

'Bunch of pig-houses,' Serge replied in his broken English.

'Slums,' Luc Valery translated.

The Balkan boy nodded. 'Like Cernograd after the shelling. Nowhere I seen before.'

'Well, I know where we are,' Matt said. 'Remember that map Rob Falk showed us? We're in the middle of the orange splotch, the houses waiting to be knocked down and turned into expensive condos. Back that way,' he jerked a thumb over his shoulder, 'is the Gardens at Carrollsburg. In the other direction, if we went far enough, is the Mall and all the museums. To the west, once you get past the parkway and the dead neighborhood, are the luxury highrises along the Potomac. East of here—' Matt frowned, trying to recall the maps he'd seen of the area. There'd been a large blank spot . . .

Then he remembered. 'The Washington Navy Yard. They haven't built a boat there in seventy years, but they use the land for offices and stuff.'

'How nice,' Luc said in a snotty voice. 'Now we know exactly where we're going to die.'

Matt shook his head. 'Only if we let that happen.'

'Let it?' Luc said. 'How do you expect to stop it? We're trapped at least four storys off the ground with no way down and bars around us—'

He was interrupted as Matt's hand shot out to grab his tie. 'Real silk?'

'W-what?' The French boy sputtered. 'My *cravat*? Yes, it's silk.'

'Heavy silk,' Matt said, yanking at the knot in the tie.

Luc said nothing. He only stared at Matt as if the American had gone out of his mind.

Matt yanked the tie free of Luc's collar, then turned to

one of the chairs. He brought it up over his head and smashed it against the wall.

'What are you doing?' Caitlin yelled. She, too had become convinced that Matt had gone out of his mind.

Matt grabbed another chair, and the other prisoners cringed back. But this one he leaned against the east side of the bell tower and began climbing.

Carrying the tie and a broken leg from the chair in one hand, Matt hauled himself up. He looped the tie around tow bars, tied it tight, then stuck the wooden stick into the loop and began twirling it. The heavy silk wrapped around the stick, making the loop tighter and tighter. Something had to give – and it wasn't the tie.

With a deep, rasping creak, the two old bars of iron began to bend together.

A second later, Serge was pulling a chair up beside Matt. He tucked another broken chair leg under his arm while he undid his belt. 'Real leather from the homeland,' he said, looping it around the bars next to where Matt was working.

The work didn't go quickly or easily. Matt's face was streaked with dust and rust as he levered against the raw wood, trying to twist his loop tighter. Serge's belt broke from the mistreatment of the leather, and they had to replace it with Matt's.

As they worked at bending the bars, the prisoners also argued over the next part of their escape. Luc had friends in the Gardens at Carrollsburg, and had visited the area several times. 'The hovercraft does not run all day,' he said. 'Last boat is at eight o'clock.' He glanced from the setting sun to his wristwatch. 'Which is not so far away. We must get to the guards at the gate and warn them!'

'If we run that way, we'll be stuck right where Rob and his pals want us,' Matt objected. 'All they have to do is move up their timetable, and we'll be trapped with all the other people in the development.'

'We should be trying to get out on the other side,' Caitlin said. 'Get the attention of the people driving on the parkway.'

'Luc and I tried that,' Serge replied. 'We shouted. I even waved my shirt. Nobody notices. They go by too fast.'

'Our one hope is the Navy Yard,' Matt insisted. 'There are military people there, and a Marine base nearby. If anyone can derail Rob's crazy plan, they're the people to do it.'

At last, they made enough headway against their prison to contemplate leaving it. The bars had been bent apart enough that a kid – even a stocky kid like Serge – could squeeze between them. Matt pushed his way through until, still clinging to the bars, he hung outside the belfry!

They were lucky that the church steeple was so short and squatty. The top of the peaked roof was about a body-length below the belfry opening.

Matt maneuvered himself around until he was hanging by his hands. He stretched out his feet, searching with his toes for a hold. There! Matt rested his weight on the questing foot. The roof tiles held. Balancing against the wall, he slid down until he was sitting astride the peak of the roof.

Matt looked up at the three worried faces peering down at him. 'So far, so good,' he reported. 'Send down the chair leg.'

Luc leaned out, extending one of the legs from the chair Matt had broken. It was an L-shaped piece of wood, with part of a bracing piece sticking out.

Matt knew the next part wouldn't be easy. The steep roof slanted down for a good two storys. If he could worm his way down to the rain gutters at the edge of the roof, he should be able to leap the rest of the way to the ground. If he lost control and slid down, he'd probably crash and break his neck.

While he'd been working on the bars, Matt had noticed that there were gaps among the roof tiles. That's why he'd brought his crude wooden hook. If he began to slide, he'd jam the hook between tiles and catch himself.

Above him, Luc was already squeezing his way out. Cat would follow, then Serge. Matt let himself down so he lay on top of the sun-warmed tiles, trying to spread his weight as widely as possible.

'Here goes,' he whispered, letting go his hold of the roof.

The angle was too steep! He began to slide down the roof tiles, faster and faster! He was out of control, and heading straight toward certain death!

Chapter 19

Once or twice, Matt had gone on virtual mountaineering adventures. He'd learned a technique called the *glissade*, where mountain climbers slide down icy glaciers using their ice axes to brake their descent. Matt had thought he could use the same technique if he got in trouble on the church roof.

Now he was finding that there was a difference between ice and roofing tile, especially when he only had a piece of shattered wood to slow himself up.

His trusty chair leg cracked and splintered as he tried to dig it in and stop his fall. When he finally caught it in a crack, it nearly jerked right out of his hands. He held on desperately, and stopped – until the tile tore loose and he was tumbling again.

He was moving a little more slowly, but the edge of the roof was coming up fast. Matt was doing his best to keep his head. With luck, he might be able to catch himself on the rain gutter at the edge.

But when he got there, the gutter was gone! Somebody must have torn it away to sell the copper sheeting.

Matt had one last chance. This part of the roof seemed to

give under his weight. He thrust down as hard as he could with his stick. The roofing gave a bit, until – finally, the wooden stick in his hands bit through. He stopped just in time – his legs were dangling over the edge.

'L-looks like one heck of a ride,' Cat Corrigan called from her place on the top of the roof.

Matt made violent shushing gestures. From his dangerous perch, he could see that the Buzzards had posted guards around the church. The one on this side was an Asian kid – what was his name? Ng?

It was not exactly like watching a military sentinel. Ng sort of slouched along the street with Willy's pistol stuck in his belt.

But Ng could pull out that gun and use it if he heard the prisoners calling to one another.

At least the others took his hint. Their heads went together, and they came up with a pretty good plan. They formed a human ladder. Serge held on at the top while Luc worked his way down until he was holding onto Luc's ankles. Then it was Caitlin's turn. She slid down, clutching at the others to keep from going too fast.

She still had to let go of Luc's feet and slide free the last six feet or so, but Matt had braced himself to catch her.

Even so, they almost went over together. Cat dangled for a heart-stopping minute. But she quickly transferred her grip to the stick dug into the roof instead of Matt's arm.

'*Pwooooh!*' she breathed long and hard. Then she spotted Ng patrolling below. 'Now I see why you wanted us to shut up,' Cat whispered.

Matt nodded.

The girl glanced uneasily from the guard to their two companions stretched across the roof. 'They can't hold on up there forever,' she whispered. Then she nodded toward the wooden hook. 'And I don't know how long this will hold, either.'

This time Matt didn't answer. He was busy watching Ng slouch along on his return march.

When the guard was under them, Matt released his hold.

Maybe he should have warned Caitlin. She gave a sort of strangled cry, which made Ng look up. The Asian boy's eyes went big, and he tried to haul the pistol from his waistband.

Then Matt landed on him. They both tumbled to the ground, but Matt was on top. This time, Ng didn't have a hostage to hold Matt frozen. Matt applied a quick but painful hold, and the gun dropped from Ng's nerveless fingers.

The other boy yelled at the top of his lungs.

Matt swore to himself. He *knew* he should have gone for a knockout blow, but he'd been too worried about that gun. Now he didn't worry about finesse. He hit, hard, and Ng flopped back, silent.

'Move! Fast!' Matt hissed, looking up at the two pairs of legs dangling over the edge of the roof. Caitlin dropped down, and Matt caught her. Luc's legs waved wildly, and then another pair appeared. Serge had made it.

They dropped together, just as a Buzzard guard came around the corner – Matt's old pal Willy.

'Yo, Ng, what's the big problem?'

The blond boy stared in astonishment at the escaping prisoners. His mouth opened to yell a warning as his right hand tore under his shirt to get his gun.

Serge snatched Ng's pistol from the ground.

The sound of the two shots seemed to blend together. Willy screamed and spun, his left hand clamping to his shoulder. Serge charged forward.

'Serge, you idiot, you're heading the wrong way!' Luc called. He, Matt, and Caitlin were already pounding down the street to the east.

Scooping up Willy's gun, Serge shouted back, 'I go to the road!'

There was no time to argue. The sound of the shots would definitely bring the Buzzards out of their staging area.

Matt risked a glimpse back as he and his companions reached the nearest street corner. Gang members came boiling out of the abandoned church like ants from a disturbed ant hill.

Then the gunfire began by the church entrance.

'Guess somebody spotted Serge,' Luc said.

But a loud, growling voice rose over the scattered shots. Matt recognized it. James was giving orders to his troops. 'Where are the others?' the gang warlord yelled. 'Find 'em! Find 'em *now*!'

Matt whipped around the corner, herding the others in front of him. 'Come on,' he said. 'They're going to have search parties out in a minute.'

'We won't even make it down this street before they get around the corner,' Caitlin said.

'So we hide.' Matt scanned the rows of houses opposite them and chose one at random. It still had a door rather than a plywood barrier or a rough wall of cinderblock across the entrance. He was afraid it might be locked, but there was neither a lock nor a doorknob. They'd been chopped out of the wooden panel, which simply swung in when he hit it with his palm.

They stepped into the shadowy interior, lit with a couple of streams of light coming from chinks in the warped plywood panels that were supposed to seal the glassless windows. Matt shut the door, peering out the chopped hole. It gave him enough of a view of the street to show gang members in their green and black Buzzards colors running down the street the escaped prisoners had just left.

'Now they'll have people ahead of us,' Luc said. 'And they have enough people left to begin a house-to-house search.'

Matt turned from the doorway. 'We'll barricade the door to slow them down. While they fool with that, we'll get out the back.'

They were in the front hallway of the old house. Obviously, a long time ago it had been cut up into apartments. To the right, a flight of stairs rose to the second floor. On the left was an apartment entrance, its door hanging at a drunken angle from broken hinges.

Matt went inside. Once this had been the front parlor, but it had been turned into a studio apartment. A soggy foam mattress squished with rainwater as Matt pulled it aside. The furniture in here had apparently been left as junk, and Matt had to agree with that assessment. Everything was cheap and shoddy. Still, enough of it held together to be potentially useful now. He wedged the rusty metal bedframe against the door. 'See what's in the next apartment,' he ordered as he started pulling a warped chipboard bookcase forward to add to the barricade.

Luc called out, 'There's an old trunk in here that must have been too heavy to carry.'

Matt had joined him, and they dragged the big, moldy leather trunk toward the door. That's when they heard Caitlin gasp. 'We've got to get out of here – and quick!' She ran back toward them, and Matt and Luc abandoned the trunk.

Caitlin led them up the hallway. This was a larger apartment, and they could see daylight coming from the doorway of a room in the distance. Light also came from a wrecked window on the air shaft, where rainwater lapped like a miniature lake. The leakage had also done a job on the hallway floor. Part of it had crumbled away, falling into the cellar below. A six-foot hole stood between them and the rear of the house!

Matt stepped toward the hole. The floor gave way sickeningly under his feet. 'We might make it with a running jump,' he said.

'Or the impact of landing might take us through the floor and down there.' Luc peered into the shadowy cellar.

What they needed was a bridge, and fast.

'The door to the front apartment!' Matt said. The three of them rushed back to the front of the house, twisting and pulling at the door to free it from its bent hinges.

Maybe the noise carried. Maybe it was just bad luck that Buzzards came to check the house. When the outside door didn't give immediately, a yell went up. Fists crashed on the old oak panel, and Matt heard more voices outside – the search party must be gathering at the doorstep.

He heaved desperately, and the door came free. 'Let's go!' he hissed, and the three of them stumbled down the hallway with the heavy door.

At the same moment, one of the gangbangers outside decided to try and shoot his way in. Pistol shots echoed down the hall and a bullet whined off the bed frame in the hastily assembled barricade.

He's seen too many holos, Matt thought. There's no lock for him to break.

Even so, other Buzzards followed their gang-brother's example. Bullets tore through the outer door and the plywood panels covering the windows. Matt, Luc, and Caitlin piled through the entrance to the rear apartment, glad to put a couple of walls between them and the firing line.

'Your barrier won't last very long against that,' Luc panted as they dragged the door past the abandoned trunk.

'What if they go through the houses on either side?' Caitlin asked. 'They could be waiting for us out back.'

'Let's hope they don't think of that right away,' Matt said. 'One problem at a time.'

Matt and Luc stood on either side of the door. They boosted it forward to cover the hole. Would it work?

Luc turned to Caitlin. 'You're the lightest. Why don't you go first?'

She simply shook her head.

Luc's lips went tight. 'We don't have time to argue.' Moving slowly and carefully, as if he were walking a tightrope, he stepped onto the makeshift bridge.

Breath hissed in between Matt's teeth. He could *see* the

floor sagging at either end of the panel. But Luc reached the far side and continued on. 'It's solid here,' he reported.

'C'mon, Caitlin,' Matt said. 'You saw that it held.'

'It *sank*,' she said in a choked voice.

There was no time for fooling around. Matt stepped onto the door-bridge. He could think of a couple of hundred things that were more fun than that simple, seven-foot stroll. Every step seemed to affect the balance of the improvised bridge and its unsteady underpinnings.

He let go a breath he hadn't realized he'd been holding when he reached the far side. Luc had already gone ahead, exploring the rear rooms. Now he came back, dragging a stinking wooden box. 'They were books, I think,' he said. 'Before the mildew got them.'

Matt's attention was on Caitlin, who still stood frozen on the wrong end of their bridge.

'Come on – now!' Matt called. 'If we made it over, you'll be okay.'

'I – I can't,' she choked.

Luc set down his burden. 'Cat, come to us,' he said. 'We cannot carry you. It would be too heavy.'

She took a baby step forward, then another.

Off toward the front of the house, they heard a splintering crash. 'Here they come,' Matt said.

It was as if he'd said the magic words. Caitlin suddenly scooted forward, her arms outstretched as if to balance herself. Although she was lighter than the boys, her sudden, jerky movements put more stress on the bridge.

Matt's jaw clenched so hard his teeth ached as he listened to the creaks and moans of rotten wood.

Cat had almost reached the far end – but the bridge was dipping!

'Anchor me,' Luc said to Matt.

Bracing himself on a solid section of flooring, Matt clamped a strong grip onto the back of Luc's pants. The French boy leaned forward, reaching out to grab the tottering Caitlin's frantically fluttering hands.

He caught her! Matt pulled backwards, dragging all three of them from the soft spot. Their bridge dangled crookedly, just a hair away from collapsing. If they hadn't managed to get Caitlin off in time . . .

They heard voices coming down the front hallway. Luc whirled round, grabbed the box of mildewed books and swept it onto the bridge. The extra weight sent the door panel crashing down into the basement.

Matt was already pulling Caitlin into the rear room, toward the windows.

There was actually glass in the frames. Matt wrestled the window open, then helped Caitlin through.

The building didn't have much of a backyard. Matt realized that the back rooms had been tacked onto the original structure. There was just a yard of two of muddy, graveled ground and a five-foot-tall wooden fence.

Matt quickly swarmed over, then reached down to help Caitlin up. Luc had caught up with them and was already scaling the boards.

There was a yard beyond the fence, ten yards of weedy, grassy, empty space before they could reach the shelter of the frame building in the distance. Someone had tried to take care of the old house. It had been painted white, with green trim around the windows.

A yell from behind showed that their pursuers had finally gotten around the grand canyon. As Matt glanced back, a head appeared over the back fence, and the flat *crack!* of a shot rang out.

Matt had a second to be glad that the gang didn't have the time or ammunition for target practice. A bullet whirred past him like an angry hornet, shattering a window in the house ahead.

Using his forearm, Matt smashed away the jagged fragments still left in the window frame and swung Cat up.

'See what's ahead,' he told the girl, sticking out a hand to Luc. He had to get the French boy in quickly. More Buzzards were appearing at the fence and clambering over.

Matt half-hauled Luc into the room, which was filled with bundles of newspapers. Matt stared in disbelief. How long had it been since the *Washington Post* came out on paper? The newsprint was brittle, flaky, and dry as tinder.

Through the window, Matt saw another Buzzard hop down from the top of the fence. This one held a rifle.

Matt squinted. The body seemed too bulky . . .

'Run!' he suddenly snapped to Luc. 'That idiot's got a grenade launcher!'

They tumbled along a twisting pathway among chest-high piles of paper, getting out of the room just as a dull *fwoomp!* announced the firing of the launcher.

A spitting canister spewed a cloud of what Matt figured was tear gas.

The guy is a double idiot, he thought, slamming the door. Tear gas might be useful in the Gardens at Carrollsburg, against people who try to hunker down in their homes. But we're not trying to stay here. We're trying to get out. And a cloud of tear gas will just slow up the pursuit.

But then he heard something more than the hiss of gas. Was that the crackle of flames?

Matt swore. The blasted grenade had set the piled papers on fire!

He ran at top speed for the front rooms.

This is a wooden house, a nervous voice chattered inside his skull. *The whole place could go up!*

Black smoke was already trailing him as he pounded along. Matt caught up with Caitlin and Luc, who were peeking out the front door.

'Fire!' Matt announced in a breathless voice. 'Out! Now!'

'But—' Caitlin began.

Matt wasn't about to argue. He threw the door open and stumbled out onto a rickety porch.

Then he saw what the others had been trying to warn him about. A quartet of searchers stood at the far end of the block.

He should have been shot down, but the Buzzards were too distracted.

He ducked back, standing flat against the wall of the old house. The back of the house they'd just emerged from was completely engulfed in flames, which shot into the sky, smearing a pillar of smoke across the red sky of sunset. Here, on the front porch, hidden in shadows, they should be invisible to the searchers.

But their safety was only temporary. Inside the house, the flames were encroaching – getting closer to them every second.

The escapees couldn't stay there much longer. Matt hoped it was dark enough – there weren't any street lights in this desolate part of town. It was time to take action – even desperate action. He took a deep breath. Maybe they wouldn't notice he wasn't wearing the gang's colors.

'Yo!' Matt yelled to the gangbangers. 'We got 'em trapped out back. Come on!' He waved toward the back of the house.

Yelling their heads off, the four heavily armed youths charged back around the corner.

Matt turned back to the doorway. Heat was pouring out of the house – along with corrosive smoke. Cat and Luc were coughing as they stumbled out, their hands smearing black stains across their mouths and chins.

Got to get out of here, Matt thought. The fire will act like a beacon for every Buzzard in the area.

He set off at a determined jog-trot, the others reeling after him. This was an east-west street. Just a few blocks, a quarter of a mile at most, and they'd reach the safety of the Navy Yard . . .

A furious shot erupted behind them. 'There he is!'

The searchers he'd scammed were back, and they'd brought plenty of friends. Matt risked a look over his shoulder. Perhaps three-quarters of a block stretched between the escapees and the gang hunting them.

They're not great shots, Matt told himself. *But there are enough of them back there, and some have automatic weapons. If we don't get out of the way, they could get lucky really fast.*

'Move!' The word came out more as a croak as he pushed his pace into a run. At least if they got around the corner . . .

Then, ahead, he saw dark, wiry figures rounding the street corners.

Matt swerved, leading his companions to the shelter of a stone stairway. He swallowed, tasting the bile flavor of blackest despair. They were cut off, pinned in front and rear by two groups of gang members who'd be delighted to kill them. They'd have been better off back in the belfry!

Chapter 20

A shouted command rang out, and all of a sudden, brilliant lights lanced through the early evening dimness. The gang-bangers ahead scuttled aside like roaches caught on the kitchen floor. The lights advanced at a walking pace. Matt made out the shapes of four Humvees, accompanied by figures on foot toting heavy rifles.

Matt caught a flash of green from the newcomers' clothing. But they weren't Buzzard reinforcements. The green came from the fatigues of U.S. Marines.

Behind the guard detail, lights flashing, was a firetruck! The driver honked his horn, eager to get on with the job of dousing the flames.

Matt suddenly found himself blessing the idiot who'd launched the grenade and set the house on fire. True, it had acted like a gigantic signal flare, drawing in all the Buzzards searching for them.

But it had also drawn the firefighting team from the Navy Yard!

And, since the fire was in a supposedly derelict area, the powers that be had sent a Marine escort in case there might be trouble.

The Buzzards had been temporarily taken by surprise. Still, they outnumbered the Marines by a good ten to one. They could try to overrun the troopers and still attempt their big knockover.

But the Humvees had to have radios. If they could warn the Marines – get the word out . . .

Matt turned to Luc and Caitlin. 'Come on. We've got to tell them what they're stepping into. What's going on.'

He stepped away from the feeble refuge of the steps and walked into the gleam of the headlights, his hands up.

Marine rifles snapped in his direction, but Matt kept walking forward, making sure his empty hands were visible. 'You've got about two hundred gang members ahead of you,' he warned. 'They've massed here—'

'For an attack on the Gardens at Carrollsburg,' Cat Corrigan interrupted, stepping past him. She, too, kept her hands in the air. 'They kidnapped my friends and me. I'm Caitlin Corrigan, the senator's daughter.'

'Smart girl,' Luc muttered.

Matt glanced at the other boy.

'Word of the kidnapping must be out by now,' Luc explained. 'The soldiers will have to take her seriously.'

Matt was about to explain that they were Marines, not soldiers, when he caught a flicker of movement out of the corner of his eye.

As the standoff developed, Rob Falk must have crept up through the shadows to the steps of the row house that the escapees had just left. Now he rose up out of his hiding place, the old M9 pistol he'd taken from Serge Woronov in his hand, his eyes glittering.

'Oh, no, bitch,' he gritted. 'You're not wrecking everything I've worked for.'

Luc took off in a wild leap to stop Falk just as the shot roared out.

Matt figured that Rob had never handled a real gun in his life. He didn't hit Caitlin. He hit Luc.

The French boy cried out, spinning and clutching his arm. He staggered, but somehow stayed upright. Then he lurched toward Falk with the stiff-legged gait of a zombie out of a horror movie. His left arm hung useless, dripping blood onto the cracked pavement.

But his right hand reached out hungrily for the gang's computer whiz. 'You – won't – hurt – Cat!' he growled in short, painful gasps.

Luc made himself a perfect target – and he was everything Rob Falk hated – a member of any in-crowd, from the land of privilege – and the land of diplomats.

Rob deflected his aim toward Luc. Matt could hear the click of rifles being locked and loaded behind him. If he didn't stop this – and now – it would mean the start of a general firefight.

He forced his tired legs into one last run, a wild dash that launched him into the air. 'Falk!' he yelled.

Matt didn't know what would happen. Rob was just an amateur at gunfighting, which meant his actions were completely unpredictable. If Rob had been a trained shot, he might have taken care of his aimed target before turning to Matt.

Instead, Rob hesitated, his aim flicking between the oncoming Luc and Matt, who was now hurtling toward him.

He didn't even have time to get a shot off before Matt tackled him. They hit the pavement with bruising force. Rob wriggled like an eel, trying to escape and shoot again. Matt held onto Falk's gun hand, grinding down on the wrist until the weapon fell from Rob's fingers.

When Matt kicked to send the pistol skidding away, Rob's free hand came up like a set of claws, going for Matt's eyes. Matt ducked, punched his opponent, then spun him around so he lay on his belly. He forced Rob's right arm behind his back and dragged him up, applying painful pressure until the bones creaked.

Rob cried out, but Matt held him on his feet, maintaining the come-along hold. He backed up, keeping Rob between him and the rest of the Buzzards. If they wanted to shoot, they'd have to risk hitting their pet genius.

Marine riflemen closed in around them. 'What's the story here?' a sergeant asked.

'I'm a Net Force Explorer,' Matt explained between gasps. 'If you contact Captain Winters through the Net Force Washington office, I think he'll vouch for me.'

He may be furious, Matt silently thought. *But he should still vouch for me.*

'This is the man with the computer know-how to breach the security system at the Gardens at Carrollsburg. Whatever you do, make sure his friends don't get him back.'

The crowd of gang members surged like a restless sea. They knew that if they lost Rob Falk, their whole plan would fall apart. But they were unwilling to go up against the rifles aimed against them by the Marines. If it had been police facing them, they might have made a try at storming the line. But not Marines.

Matt had finally backed up to the parked Humvees. He gave a sigh of relief as he saw a Marine lieutenant on the mobile radio. In the distance, they already heard the skirl of oncoming sirens.

After the sergeant passed on Matt's message and the lieutenant contacted Net Force, helicopters were soon in the air overhead as well.

It was over.

Inside the rectory of the abandoned church, Captain Winters shook his head. A full Net Force criminal investigation tech team was at work, going over the weirdly mismated system Rob Falk had put together.

Matt had been right. Without Falk, James and his warriors had been unable to pull off their big robbery. James himself had been on the other side of the desolate zone, leading his people in a gunfight against Serge Woronov. The Balkan diplomat's son hadn't made it to the elevated parkway. But he'd taken refuge among the concrete pilings, trading shots with James and a crew of Buzzards.

Serge had actually been wounded and was down to his last two bullets when the cops had arrived. James had fled in inglorious retreat, along with his gang. An all-points-bulletin was out on them.

The other gangbangers had tried to vanish, but police, Marines, and Net Force operatives had rounded most of them up. Some of the Buzzards had held onto their guns, others had ditched them. One thing was sure. The gang's fighting force had taken a major hit this evening.

Captain Winters came over to Matt. 'Our people are finding unbelievable things on those wired-together hard drives,' he said. 'But then, there were a lot of things in this whole case that I'd have never believed.'

It wasn't much of an apology for not listening to Matt's earlier theories about the virtual vandals. But frankly, it was more than Matt had expected.

'Then, on the other hand, I would never have expected you to take such an irresponsible, dangerous . . . downright *stupid* course of action,' Winters went on. 'Singlehandedly going undercover with no backup and no way to communicate – who do you think you are? The Spawn?'

'Captain, I left a datascrip with everything I knew on it. It had everything I found out—' Matt began, but Winters cut him off.

'If you only knew how many gravestones *that* could be carved on! We found your file after you went AWOL from school, Hunter.' He gave Matt a glare that could have melted steel. 'It was useless because Falk and the other vandals had already disappeared. The real nitty-gritty stuff that we'd need to save you, you didn't find out until you were a prisoner, now did you?'

'But I did escape, Captain,' Matt pointed out. 'I used the training I got in Net Force Explorers to get out of there.'

'Oh, yes, I heard all about your adventures from Woronov and Valery while they were being patched up.' Winters hesitated for a second. 'And from Ms Corrigan.' He shook his head again. 'Some of those lamebrain stunts – you've certainly proved one thing, Hunter. A little knowledge *is* a dangerous thing, especially if *you're* trying to apply it.'

Winters sighed. 'I guess there's only one thing to do about it. We'll have to sign you up for advanced Net Force training, if only to keep you off the streets.'

'Sir?' Matt couldn't believe his ears. Advanced training, or 'boot camp,' as the Net Force Explorers called it, was usually reserved for guys years older than he was. It would probably require his parents' approval. But he thought he'd be able to convince his mom, and she'd talk to his dad.

'Thank you, Captain,' he said.

'Don't thank me,' Winters told him. 'By the time you're through, you'll probably think you're going through the tortures of the damned. I'm just hoping it takes care of all that excess energy you seem to have.'

Matt could feel his face getting red. 'Nothing happened between Cat – Caitlin – and myself.'

'Nothing, huh? Other than getting kidnapped and shot at? I see that you decided to protect her once you knew she was involved in this mess.'

Matt shrugged, his face going redder. 'I did what I thought was right – at the time.'

'So did Luc Valery, I guess,' Winters said shrewdly.

'Yeah. I saw him talking to Cat. He finally made up his mind about whether he really liked her.'

'Not that it will do him much good,' Winters said. 'The Valerys, the Woronovs, and the Savages will all be returning to their respective countries. The State Department is already pulling the necessary strings. And, unless I miss my guess, Senator Corrigan will probably lock his daughter in a closet until she turns about thirty.'

Matt gave a ghost of a grin. No more pictures of Cat Corrigan in the society holos. That would be a switch!

'We do have a promise, however, that she'll testify – if it becomes necessary.'

That made Matt grow more serious. 'What's going to

happen to Rob Falk?' he asked.

Now it was Winters' turn to shrug. 'He's in custody, under continuous observation so he won't . . . do anything to himself. Certainly, he'll have to face a psych evaluation. The tech people here tell me he truly is a genius. But he was also ready to do some pretty bad things—'

'Including murder,' Matt finished grimly.

Captain Winters didn't disagree. He simply started talking about another subject. 'I think the federal government is going to start taking more of an interest in these ring-town gangs. They're a problem for other cities besides Washington.'

'And that will probably be the only visible result of everything that happened,' Matt said.

'After State, the FBI, and a couple of other agencies – including Net Force – are done, I suppose so.' Winters looked at Matt. 'Were you expecting a medal?'

'No!' Matt said, surprised.

'Then look at it this way. You helped avoid a four-way international incident, saved a lot of people from some very rough treatment at the hands of the Buzzards . . . and kept some very nasty technology out of some very dirty hands. Unfortunately, only a handful of people will know what you did to avert a major disaster.'

'And in return, I get a chance to bust my butt on advanced training,' Matt said.

Captain Winters nodded. 'The best possible punishment for success – it's the Net Force way. You got a problem with that?'

Matt found a slow grin creeping across his face. He shrugged. 'I guess I can live with that, Captain,' he said.